THE WISEMANN ORIGINALS

by the same author

A Graveyard of My Own

THE WISEMANN ORIGINALS

Ron Goulart

Walker and Company
New York

Copyright © 1989 by Ron Goulart

All the characters and events portrayed in this story are fictitious.

First published in the United States of America in 1989
by Walker Publishing Company, Inc.

Published simultaneously in Canada by Thomas Allen & Son
Canada, Limited, Markham, Ontario.

Library of Congress Cataloging-in-Publication Data

Goulart, Ron, 1933–
The Wisemann originals / Ron Goulart.
p.   cm.
ISBN 0-8027-5722-7
I. Title.
PS3557.085W57   1989
813'.54 – dc19   88-28681
CIP

Printed in the United States of America

10 9 8 7 6 5 4 3 2 1

1

NAVARRO WAS RUNNING along the warm morning beach, barefoot and seemingly carefree, when his beeper started to beep.

He clicked it off and continued his steady trot over the sand and seaweed. Navarro wasn't especially fond of running, but he'd resolved to do two miles each and every day. He'd been improving himself for nearly five months now, ever since his wife had gone away.

Thirty-one years old and at least three or four inches shorter than he had hoped to be as a kid, Navarro was wearing a fairly new pair of gray warmup pants and a T-shirt whose clever remark had long since faded. The shirt had been given him by his erstwhile wife. Navarro's hair was dark and curly and whenever he exerted himself, as he was doing now, it tended to stand up and give the impression he'd just unexpectedly clutched a live wire.

The placid, blue Pacific stretched away to infinity on his left, three sooty seagulls circled high above, and a pedigreed cocker spaniel was worrying a huge hunk of driftwood down at the water's edge.

When Navarro spotted the red-haired airline hostess in the green bikini doing her exercises out on her redwood sundeck, he slowed and halted. She was his daily landmark, indicating he'd run just about a mile from his own beach house. The long, tan redhead ceased her toe-touching and turned to wave at him across the thirty yards of sunny beach that separated them.

"*Buenos días,*" she called, smiling.

"Big tits and bilingual, too," said Navarro, nowhere near loud enough for her to hear. He grinned, tipped an imaginary hat to her, then commenced running back toward home.

His phone was ringing when he trudged, panting some, into his large, low-key living room. Navarro ignored the phone, which sat in the exact center of his blonde coffee table, and made his way to the bathroom.

Glancing at himself in the mirror over the sink, he remarked, "I thought Chico Marx was dead."

After a long shower, during which he sang the best parts of several Mexican jukebox hits he'd learned during his youth up in the San Joaquin Valley, Navarro went into his redwood-paneled bedroom and dressed. He'd made the bed before going out and there wasn't so much as a discarded sock on the gray carpeting. He put on a tan suit, which he felt went well with his red and white rugby shirt. Deciding against wearing his .38 revolver, Navarro went into his kitchen. From among the neat rows of containers inside the spotless blue refrigerator he chose a carton of plain yogurt.

He carried that, along with a paper napkin and a red plastic spoon, back into the living room. Seated on the long low sofa, he ate six spoonfuls without much enthusiasm. "I wish to hell self-improvement tasted better," he said, putting the container and the spoon down on a napkin.

After rubbing his fingertips together, safecracker fashion, he picked up the phone and punched out a number, then watched the pale blue ocean outside his wide front window.

After three rings, a pleasant, feminine voice answered with, "Ajax Novelty Company. Good morning."

"Good day, sir or madam. This is Dial-A-Crank and we're inquiring if you'd like to subscribe to a month of heavy breathing."

"Morning, Navarro. Where the dickens have you been? I've been trying to get you for an hour."

"It's the oddest thing, Emmy Lou. I awoke to find myself in this sepulchre. Some guys rolled away the stone at the entrance. They mentioned something about resurrection."

"Are you up to a new assignment?"

"Why shouldn't I be?"

Out on the ocean a gleaming white cabin cruiser was easing by, aimed for Mexico.

2

"That last case, three weeks ago — those truck hijackers almost broke your arm."

"Almost doesn't win a cigar. I'm fine."

"I worry about you. Did you know that?"

"All women worry about me. It has something to do with my innate cuteness. What's the new job?"

"I mean, a lot of these investigations of ours put you up against some rough people. Rough *and* big. You're sort of a shrimp, and —"

"I live by my wits and cunning," Navarro told her. "What's the job?"

"Well, it sounds sort of dippy, but Wexler says it's exactly the kind of thing Ajax is noted for tackling."

"Details," he requested.

"You're supposed to get out to the San Fernando Valley. In fact — I'm looking at my watch — you're going to have to hustle. You have an appointment with Mr. Joel Kingsmark at —"

"Paradine Pictures. This isn't another nitwit actor on drugs, is it?"

"No, no. Art treasures or something like that. And you're probably going to have to travel around the country a bit."

"What time am I supposed to see this fabled movie mogul?"

"Eleven forty-five. Can you make it?"

"Sure."

"I worry about you racing along the freeways in that clunky old Volkswagen of yours. The money you make, you could afford a Mercedes."

"I'd rattle around inside a big car. Does Wexler want to see me after I talk to Kingsmark?"

"You're not angry because I alluded to you as a shrimp?"

"The truth never hurts, Em. Does he?"

"Yes, at four he says. But make it four-thirty, you know him."

"Alas, yes."

He hung up, but stayed on the sofa for a moment, staring out at the Pacific Ocean. "Wonder if this is one I can use Briggs on."

Some three thousand miles to the east, Jack Briggs awoke

without even a faint premonition that Navarro was soon to come popping back into his life. He felt bad enough as it was.

He came to sprawled across the half of the bed Ann had occupied up until three weeks ago. His eyes felt as if they were encrusted with the burning sands of the Sahara, while various parts of his skull throbbed in waltz time.

When Briggs, who was the same age as Navarro but a good six inches taller, rolled out of bed, his inner workings made protesting gurgles. In response to that protest, he stayed on his hands and knees on the floor for a spell, swaying gently alongside the pile of rumpled clothing that looked vaguely like what he'd worn last night.

"At least I don't have the world's worst hangover this time," he muttered. "I'd rate this only the fourth or fifth worst."

Briggs took several slow, open-mouthed breaths but felt no better. Managing a shaky pushup, he got himself upright.

The digital clock, which sat on his bedside table amid secondhand Kleenexes, a half a bag of Oreo cookies, seven science fiction paperbacks and an overflowing ashtray, informed him it was 11:16 A.M. Briggs felt especially bad about the ashtray. Since he didn't smoke, the cigarette butts piled high in it must be Ann's. He should've emptied them long since.

He worked his way across the bedroom, walking over old copies of the New York *Times.* He wasn't up to checking himself out in the streaked mirror above his bureau just yet. Sitting atop the bureau in lazy rows, some of them leaning against each other like sick old men, were his trophies. The whole lot was dusty, some festooned with cobwebs. Most of them dated back to college. Imagine hauling the damn things all over the country for eleven years or more. He'd earned the college ones in boxing, the later ones mostly for running in minimarathons in Manhattan. He'd gone through two marriages, four live-ins and five art director jobs since winning the last one.

And there were those who claimed he never got anything accomplished.

Running his tongue over his teeth, which gave him gooseflesh, Briggs wandered into the small yellow kitchen.

He opened the refrigerator and saw a half a pizza staring out at him. Judging by the look of it, this was a pepperoni-and-green-scum pizza. Briggs grabbed a can of beer off a shelf, shut the box and seated himself, gingerly, at the kitchen table.

The dishes from last night were still on the table, along with the Help Wanted section from last Sunday's *Times*. Setting his beer can next to the dinner plate, Briggs picked up a ballpoint pen that had come to rest in a nearly empty margarine tub.

His phone rang.

Briggs got up, cautiously, and crossed to the wall unit. "Hello," he said in a chipper voice.

He was expecting calls from a few of the ad agencies where he'd dropped off his resumé and shown his sample portfolio.

"Um…," came a tentative male voice.

"Ah, Mr. Thompson," said Briggs in a smiling tone. "Don't tell me that check of mine hasn't reached you yet?"

"I don't like to bother you at a time like this, Mr. Briggs," said the credit manager of one of Manhattan's large department stores.

For a few seconds Briggs thought old Thompson had somehow heard about Ann's moving out. Then he recalled he'd told him last week that he was just recovering from a bout of pleurisy. "No, that's okay. I'm feeling pretty well, all things considered. What really upsets me, though, is what could have happened to that darn check."

"How much was it for, did you say?"

"Just a second. I've got it right here in my check register." Briggs gazed up at the sooty ceiling. "Right, here she is. Check #8067 for the amount of $79.82. That's the whole amount I owe you, I believe."

"Well, yes, except for the additional late charge of $2.50."

"Gee, I don't feel I ought to be charged that, since I did mail the check to you people over ten days ago. Boy, the postal system in New York City is the world's worst."

"Suppose you stop payment and send us a new check, Mr. Briggs?"

"I suppose I could do that. Okay, Mr. Thompson, if you don't get that check by next week at this time, be sure and let me know," said Briggs, letting concern show in his voice. "Despite what my doctor says, I'm sure I'll be able to hobble into your store by then and hand you a new check."

"If it doesn't arrive by the day after tomorrow, Mr. Briggs, I'll be in touch again."

Hanging up, he leaned against the kitchen wall. "Jesus," he said. "How'd I get to be the world's biggest deadbeat?"

Returning to the table, he picked up the can of beer. It was perhaps too early in the day for drinking. He shrugged, opened the can, and took a long swallow.

2

THE AJAX NOVELTY Company offices were twenty-two stories above one of the more civilized stretches of the Sunset Strip. At about ten minutes shy of four, Navarro came strolling into the chill, off-white and pale gold reception room. He was finishing up, without much enthusiasm, a health-food candy bar whose chief ingredient was alfalfa sprouts.

At the far end of the room Emmy Lou Spraden was seated behind a teakwood desk reading the second volume of the three-volume edition of *Remembrance of Things Past*. She was twenty-nine, blonde, and too tall for Navarro.

"The baron did it," he said, coming to a halt beside her desk.

Smiling, she slid a Garfield bookmark between the pages of the fat book and shut it. "Did you see Kingsmark?"

"Yep, he granted me an audience."

"What's he like?"

"He has impressive teeth. Did you get the information I phoned you about?"

Her slightly freckled nose wrinkled. "Yes, but you aren't intending to use your friend Briggs again, are you?"

"Matter of fact, I am. If he's available."

Emmy Lou sighed. "Oh, he's available, sure enough." Opening one of the manila folders scattered on her desk top, she extracted several sheets of printout paper. "This came in from New York about an hour ago."

Navarro rested his left buttock against the desk and scanned the sheets. "*Chihuahua*," he remarked after a couple of minutes. "I try to keep up with him, but I didn't know most of this."

"Nothing unexpected for Briggs, is it? He's just gone through another wife and a couple more jobs since you used him to help you on that art forgery case three years ago."

"Was it that long?" Shaking his head, Navarro folded the pages neatly in half.

Emmy Lou tapped her fingertips on the closed volume of Proust. "You've known him for a long time, right?"

"Since college, up at Berkeley."

"And you've remained friends all this time."

"Sure, even though we don't see each other too often anymore. Some friendships just seem to last no matter what. It's like Butch Cassidy and the Sundance Kid, or —"

"More like Laurel and Hardy," Emmy Lou said. "I admit Briggs is an expert when it comes to art and drawing matters, but he did kind of foul up on that forgery job."

"Only around the edges." Navarro straightened up. "Well, I'd better see Wexler."

The blonde was watching his face. "Don't get angry with me if I say something, okay?"

"Give me a second to get a rein on my fiery temper. All righty, go ahead."

"I'm serious."

"Me, too. Just yesterday somebody called me dour. Speak."

She took a deep breath. "Well, you've got a...a stray dog complex. You're always trying to help out the lame and the halt. That's no way for a private investigator to be."

"Ever since I saw *Gandhi* on cable I can't help myself."

"No, really. I honestly think...well, the same thing was true about your wife. Doris Beestinger or whatever her dippy name was. She —"

"Doris Biesecker."

"Whatever. You have to admit that Doris was sort of...well, not the most stable person when you met her four years ago. Then you took her in, were overwhelmingly supportive and all. She improved, blossomed, and then left you."

Navarro took a step back from the desk. "Is Wexler handy?"

"You mad at me?"

8

He gave her a grin. "Outraged, ticked off, and seething with resentment, but hardly mad at all."

"The point that I'm trying to make," she said carefully, "is I think Briggs is another one of your stray dogs."

"Could be you're absolutely right, Em."

"So what are you going to do?"

"Try to hire Briggs to help me out on this one," answered Navarro.

Navarro shifted in the chair, fighting against the temptation to neaten up the clutter on his boss's desk. "I'd rather use Briggs," he said again.

Courtney Wexler, head of the Ajax Novelty Company, was a husky, slope-shouldered man of fifty. His hair was close-cropped and graying over his ears. His tweedy sport coat had a thick leather patch at each elbow.

"I think I know what your problem is," he said across the welter of folders, memos and miscellaneous clutter.

"*Chihuahua*, everybody seems to know my problem. Did the government issue a White Paper about my innermost—"

"How come you keep peppering your conversation with those B-movie Chicano expressions?"

"*Caramba*, Court, it's my Hispanic heritage showing through," he replied. "Besides, when I was a kid I watched a lot of *Cisco Kid* reruns. In fact, that was all we could get on TV in my neighborhood. That and Ricardo Montalban commercials."

"I happen to have a whole list of perfectly fine graphics experts right here someplace," said Wexler, feeling around among his papers. "Including two in the Florida area, where you'll be going initially on this new assignment. All you have to do is get one of them to take a look at the drawings in question, when and if you locate them. It's simple. You don't need a lush from Manhattan working full time."

"Give me the name of one of your experts."

Wexler continued his search for the list. "As I recall, one of them is a university professor, or used to be. Professor James Fennimore Ivey. Very much respected and an expert on European pen-and-ink artists of the first half of the twentieth century."

Navarro scratched at his curly hair. "How old is he?"

"I'm not sure. His title is Professor Emeritus, so I assume he's — "

"An old coot."

"His eyesight hasn't failed. You show him a good clear photocopy of one of these drawings, and he'll be able to tell you if it's authentic or not. Then you get back on the trail of the possible cache. It's a cinch."

"People have been getting killed down there in Florida."

Shaking his head, Wexler held up a single finger. "One guy is dead. And that was most likely an accident that has nothing to do with this case."

"Briggs knows as much about graphics as your doddering prof, and he's more help in a fight."

"We're not anticipating violence."

"Neither was Kingsmark's gopher."

Wexler rubbed at his left elbow patch. "When we hired Briggs as a consultant before, he did some embarrassing things."

"What the hell is embarrassing about a brawl?"

"In an art gallery it's inappropriate."

"We proved those damn paintings were fakes. We caught the guys who produced them. That saved the insurance company a million bucks and put a hundred thousand in the Ajax coffers."

"True," admitted his boss. "The thing is, Briggs simply isn't dependable."

"Look." Navarro leaned forward. "If you wanted to run a completely strait-laced, conservative detective agency, you'd have named this operation the Wexler Detection Service, not the Ajax Novelty Company."

"That was eleven years ago. I was more whimsical back then."

"Bullshit. Our reputation is still based on being unorthodox," Navarro told him. "That's why Kingsmark came to us and not to Pinkerton or Burns. We handle the odd cases, we hire operatives on a short-term basis who have just the right abilities for specific, special jobs. Hell, Ajax netted over three million dollars last year."

"I can't," said Wexler quickly, "give you another raise."

"Keep the money." Navarro grinned. "I'd like to hire Briggs. He's got the abilities to help out on this one."

Wexler rubbed at his right elbow patch. "He's living back in New York, isn't he?"

"Yep, and fortunately he's at liberty. I can sign him up for sure."

"You intend to go to Manhattan first, to gather up Briggs?"

"Then we speed down to Florida."

"These drawings that may have surfaced down there," said Wexler, "they're really valuable?"

"According to Kingsmark, and to what I've been able to find out since I chatted with him."

After rocking a few times in his swivel chair, Wexler said, "Deep down inside you really do believe you'll be able to salvage Briggs eventually, don't you?"

"Maybe, eventually."

"Touching, a friendship like that. But I don't want him to screw up an assignment like this one."

"He won't, trust me." Navarro tapped his fist against his chest. "I have a feeling Briggs is just right to help out with the Kingsmark problem."

"Briggs I'll never quite trust," said his boss, "but your instincts have been pretty reliable so far. Go ahead and hire him."

3

WHEN NAVARRO CAUGHT up with Briggs, he was making a fool of himself, at a few minutes beyond seven in the evening, in a crowded, shadowy Manhattan bar called Alfie's Pub. Briggs was standing in the smoke-blurred crowd at the far end of the room and addressing a strikingly beautiful young woman with blonde, silky hair and a small, but provocative, bosom. His quiet, expensive gray suit looked as though he had just fallen down in it, and his narrow paisley tie was draped over his shoulder.

"You're not being at all rational about this, Ann," Briggs was saying as he swayed toward and then away from the lovely blonde.

Very quietly, the young woman replied, "Take a leap for yourself, Jack."

"Hey, is that any way to talk to me? After all, we mean a lot to each other."

"You don't mean dipshit to me," she informed him.

"Ann." Briggs took hold of her handsome bare arm. "That's a nice tan you've picked up, by the way. Been on a—"

"Take your leprous hands off me, or I'll kick you in the privates."

"C'mon, Jack. Let's exit." Navarro had managed to reach his side.

Briggs blinked, the dregs of ice in his glass jiggling. "Rudy?" Chuckling, he tilted in his direction.

"The same," he said. "Let's take us a stroll outside."

"Rudy Navarro." Briggs chuckled again. "I haven't seen you in three damn years or more. And then you come walking right into Alfie's here while I'm having a spat with—Ann, do you know who this is?"

"He looks like a little Latino faggot to me," she replied.

13

Grinning, Navarro shook his head in wonderment. "Now I know what I've been missing by not being in New York. The clever badinage."

"This is Rudy Navarro," Briggs told her. "He and I used to be roommates back in — "

"It figures." She took a sip of her white wine.

"No, no, this was ten, twelve years ago," Briggs tried to explain. "In college. University of California at Berkeley. In those days, Ann, it was perfectly okay to live with a guy if you were another guy. California wasn't as queer then as it — "

"I do wish," requested the handsome young fellow on the other side of Ann, "you'd keep your offensive remarks to yourself."

"He can't help it," said Ann. "He's got a genetic defect that renders him obnoxious."

"Are you taking all this in, Rudy?" Briggs gave a bitter chuckle. "Ann and I lived together until...three weeks ago? Right, three long, sad weeks ago. Then, mind you, on the same fateful day I lost my job as Associate Art Director at Dummler, Kearsarg, Hamlin and Weirsbecky...I can't be in too bad shape if I can still reel that off. I always pitied the poor switchboard girls who had to answer the phone with that every blessed...Where was I?"

"Up shit creek," suggested Ann.

"Tossed out in the cold by Dummler, Kearsarg...and the rest of 'em. Deserted on that selfsame day by the only woman on earth I've ever truly loved."

"That is tragic," agreed the still grinning Navarro. "Now let's withdraw. I have to talk to you about something."

"I can't right yet, Rudy, because I have to persuade Ann what a tragic mistake she — "

"You two only lived together?" Navarro asked the young woman. "You weren't married?"

She scowled. "You don't think I'd be insane enough to enter into any sort of legal relationship with this baboon? I was getting over dental surgery when I first met him, and the codeine must've affected my judgment."

Nodding sympathetically, Navarro said, "Some of them he

14

marries. Those I feel worse about dragging him away from."

"You make me sound like a damn bluebird...Bluebeard. I've only had three wives thus far. So has most everybody else in Manhattan."

"Four," corrected Navarro. "Now say *adiós* to everybody."

"Four? Oh, you're counting Elana. But her folks had that annulled, so technically she doesn't figure in the total."

"What exactly do you want him for?" Ann asked Navarro. "Not that I give a rat's ass."

"A business deal."

"He's not quite as bestial and scummy if you keep him off the sauce."

"I know." Navarro nudged his friend in the side. "Begin wending your way toward the door."

"What line of work are you in?" asked Ann. "Advertising, like him?"

"No, it isn't advertising."

"He's a detective," said Briggs, fairly loudly. "A private eye."

A few of the nearest patrons in the smoky pub seemed to flinch and turn away.

"That's fascinating." Ann rubbed the rim of her wine glass across her chin. "Detective work has always seemed a fascinating field."

"I'm not actually a detective." Navarro gave her one of his most disarming grins.

"Oh, I'm sorry. I was just thinking I might need a detective sometime and I was going to ask you for your card."

"Keep this one." From the breast pocket of his dark blue suitcoat Navarro withdrew a business card. "I order them a thousand at a time."

Her lovely, tan brow furrowed slightly. "All this says is Ajax Novelty Company. There isn't even a phone number."

"Yes," agreed Navarro. He took hold of Briggs's elbow and thrust him into the cocktail crowd.

"Did you notice how Ann warmed up to you?" said Briggs as he made his stumbling way to the exit. "It's always been like that, even back at Cal. Here I am taller, smarter and better looking than you, and yet you always win out with women."

"The lady's right. You are an asshole when you're drunk."

"Me? Simply because I have a tendency to tell nothing but the truth when I've had a...Hey, why did you tell Ann you're not a detective? Aren't you anymore? I haven't seen hair nor hide of you in three, or is it four...Aren't you?"

"I still am, yeah. But I feel no need to have you making public service announcements about the fact."

A small, well-placed shove in the back propelled Briggs out into the spring twilight. Briggs paused on the sidewalk, swaying some, to watch a plump lady in furs clean up after her poodle.

"That's a symbol," he observed. "That's what we all devote our lives to, cleaning up somebody else's shit."

"Very profound. Start heading for your apartment on Lex."

"How come you know where I live? I haven't laid eyes on you since that time you conned me into working with you on that phony masterpiece thing. Where we both almost got killed."

"I know many things. The most heartening thing I know about you is you were bounced from your latest art director job and are still unemployed."

"What's so damn heartening about that? Have you, Rudy, ever stood in an employment line? It's degrading and..." Briggs stopped still again. "This isn't a coincidence at all, is it? Your running into me and everything."

"There are no coincidences in life, *amigo.*"

"No, of course not, you sneaky bastard. You found out I wasn't working and somehow it fits into some sly scheme of yours," accused Briggs. That's one more thing I remember about you. Women dote on you, and you never look me up unless you need something. You're the world's sneakiest guy."

Navarro nodded at the window of the narrow antique shop they were halted in front of. "Look at your reflection."

Briggs made a careful turn. "My tie's askew," he noted, straightening it. "Otherwise —"

"Otherwise you're about two steps from being a hopeless case," Navarro told him. "Four times married, ten times fired from advertising agencies, drunk before sundown, fighting with bimbos in saloons, going from bad to worse."

"Ann's no bimbo, she went to school in Vermont."

"We've been friends for nearly fifteen years." Navarro bounced on his heels. "I'm tired of watching you go down the drain."

"So?"

"So I'm going to make another try at helping you reform."

"You only try to shape me up when it serves you and the Ajax Novelty Company."

"Maybe so, but I think there's more to it than that," said Navarro. "I'm hoping this time, Jack, you can help me and maybe pull yourself together at the same time."

Briggs laughed. "You sound like you've been born again."

"This isn't religion. I'm talking about your ceasing to be a drunken asshole."

"I'm not an alcoholic or anything. Nine out of ten nights I never have more than a few social...Whoa, now." He pointed an accusing finger at his friend. "We're straying from the main subject. What is it you're trying to lure me into this time?"

Navarro nodded his head twice, then said, "Okay, let me ask you a question."

"Go ahead."

"Do you know who Heinrich Wisemann was?"

Briggs straightened up. "Of course. He was one of the best German pen-and-ink artists of the 1920s and 1930s," he answered. "As a satirical artist I think the guy was right up there between George Grosz and Heinrich Kley someplace. I did my Master's thesis on the German and Austrian artists who worked on *Jugend* and magazines like that."

"So I recalled. You can spot this guy's work when you see it?"

"Sure, anyone with any sense can."

"I can't. Probably nobody else back at Alfie's can."

"Everybody watches television when they ought to be doing better things," said Briggs. "What the hell does Wisemann have to do with anything?"

"I thought of you right off when this job came up," said his friend. "Lucky for me you're free at the moment. We can work together for a few weeks, or however long it takes."

"How much will it pay?"

"Well, our client's paying Ajax a hundred thousand."

"A hundred thousand?"

"Our share will be around ten thousand dollars each."

Briggs stroked his cheek. "Even so, Rudy, ten thousand is more than I made in three months as an art director at DKH&W."

"Yeah, I'm aware," said Navarro. "Now let's adjourn to your place so I can explain all this to you."

Navarro and Briggs had been walking along a dimly lit side street, going from Third Avenue over to Lexington. It was mostly lined with closed boutiques and gourmet shops. The only two apartment buildings were entirely dark in the newly arrived night.

Navarro sensed them first. "Trouble, maybe," he said quietly.

"Hum?" asked Briggs, slowing.

"Up in the doorway of that cheese shop, about a hundred yards ahead of us," his friend said, not nodding. "Three lads lurking."

"Could just be some friendly drug dealing. But let's cross the street anyway." Briggs started to step between two parked cars.

When Navarro turned to follow, the three young men left the shadows of the doorway. Above the noise of the traffic back on Third you could hear their shuffling footfalls.

"Wait a minute, mister," one of them called to him.

They were middle-sized but husky, in their early twenties at most. White, blond-haired, decked out in dark jeans and T-shirts. The tallest and meanest-looking wore a Levi jacket as well.

"Can you help us out?" he called. "We need bus fare home."

Briggs was waiting in the gutter. "Want to try to run, Rudy?"

Navarro dropped his hand into his coat pocket. "We're both pretty good runners I guess, but I don't think we have time to try that."

"Are you into running now?"

"Tell you about it at a later date."

"Hey, mister," said the meanest-looking one. "I'm talking to

18

you, you greasy little son of a bitch. Didn't you hear me ask you nice for money?"

Navarro grinned at the trio, which was circling him where he stood on the night sidewalk. "You fellows have made a mistake," he told them evenly. "Go away before anything happens."

"Don't you understand English, you spick mother? I'm asking you for money." The one with the jacket eased closer to Navarro, left hand outstretched. "You going to help out or not?"

"Nope." Navarro's eyes narrowed.

"I think you're wrong, spick." A knife appeared in his right hand. He lunged.

Navarro had been expecting that. He wasn't where he was supposed to be when the lunge ended.

From his pocket he produced a worn blackjack. As he dodged the knife blade, he swung out with the thing.

"Holy shit!" complained the attacker. "You broke my frigging hand."

The fingers of his right hand were spread wide and the knife had hit the pavement. Briggs, meanwhile, had succeeded in decking one of the other two. He was back on the sidewalk, tussling with the second one now.

Navarro tapped his blackjack in the palm of his hand. "Maybe you recall I advised you about going away, *amigo*?" he asked the one in the jacket, who was massaging his already swelling wrist.

"Shit, I got all kinds of broken bones. I can feel it."

"Depart," mentioned Navarro.

The young man pivoted on his heel, gave Navarro a mean look, threw him the finger with his good hand and then started running away.

Grinning, Navarro leaned back against the nearest car to watch Briggs and the remaining youth.

Briggs faked a left and delivered two right jabs into the young man's midsection. The youth howled, doubled up and stumbled back. He started vomiting on the curb.

Stooping, Navarro scooped up the fallen knife. "Good night, all," he said to the survivors.

Resuming their walk, Briggs said, "I didn't do too badly."

"Hell, you got two out of three."

"Yeah, considering the fact I'm heartbroken, hungover and mildly sauced, I...hey, wait now." He eyed Navarro. "This wasn't some kind of goddamn test, was it? So you could see if I have any of my old boxing skill left?"

"I don't run tests with real weapons," Navarro assured him. "But I am glad to find out you're still handy with your dukes."

Laughing, Briggs rubbed at the knuckles of his right hand. "It is sort of heartening," he admitted.

4

BRIGGS GOT UP off the kitchen floor. "What an odd place for the instant coffee to have gotten to." He kneed shut the door to the sink cabinet.

"I'll pass on the coffee." Navarro was noting the collection of dirty dishes massed in the sink.

"Was figuring on making coffee to help me sober up. But that little fracas in the street appears to have done that." Briggs made his way to his narrow electric stove, where a saucepan of water was commencing to bubble. "Ow."

"What?"

"Some noodles left over in this water. I was attempting to flick them out."

Navarro shook his head. "You've got enough green slime and gunk growing on your dishes to make your own 1950s horror flick."

Briggs dumped two spoons of instant coffee into a Styrofoam cup and added boiling water, succeeding in excluding all but one of the noodles. "You sure you don't want me to fix you some?"

"I've given it up." Navarro went out into the small living room.

"Quit coffee, gone into running. That's interesting." Holding the coffee cup in both hands, he followed.

"It is." Navarro shoved a pile of girlie magazines and dirty underwear off the sofa and sat. "But right now I'd rather talk about why I came here to recruit you."

Down on Lexington brakes squealed.

Briggs sat on the edge of his lame coffee table. "First off, let me reiterate that I'm not usually drunk and disorderly these days," he said after trying the coffee. "You just happened to encounter me at a moment when I was behaving in a somewhat foolish way."

"Somewhat."

"Ann brings that out in me," Briggs went on. "It's difficult to explain why I'm so taken with her. She isn't the most intellectual woman in the world. She has, as you may have noticed, a nasty side."

"She has very nice tits."

Briggs drank some more coffee, avoiding the floating spinach noodle. "Now that you mention it, Rudy, that is just about her only positive feature," he said. "Explain to me how we're going to make this ten thousand each."

Nodding at the stuffed bookcases, the smaller, darker man said, "I need somebody who knows all about Heinrich Wisemann. You've always been a nut about that sort of illustrator, so I thought of you."

"Three years I don't hear a blooming word from you. Not even a Christmas card. And now you come out of the blue to — "

"Merry Christmas," said Navarro. "Have you ever heard of Ralph Coulthard?"

"Sure, he was a small-time publisher in the late 1940s and early 1950s," Briggs answered, starting to rise. "Matter of fact, he did a couple of books that reprinted some of Wisemann's best work from *Simplicissimus* and *Jugend.*"

"I've already seen the books and gone over them, if that's what you're about to fetch."

"Nice books." He sat down. "I have both of 'em."

People were yelling threats and curses at each other down in the street.

"You know what supposedly happened to Wisemann," said Navarro.

"He was a Jew. Hitler got hold of him in 1940 and stuck him in a concentration camp."

"Dachau. Wisemann seems to have died there in 1943."

"That's what it says in the introduction to one of the Coulthard books."

"What would you say an original drawing by Wisemann would be worth?"

Briggs answered, "When the Marschall Gallery here in New York auctioned two of them off a year or so ago, one brought ten thousand and the other eighty-five hundred. I really liked the smaller one, with those terrific dancing alligators of his and a great horny centaur playing a mandolin and chasing a naked lady. That's the worst thing, Rudy, about not being rich. I don't miss fancy cars or gourmet food, but once in a while a drawing comes along that I really yearn for."

"If one Wisemann original is worth, say, ten thou," continued Navarro, "then two hundred and forty-one of them ought to be worth at least something in the neighborhood of two million bucks. Our client thinks so and he's willing—"

"The steamer trunk!" Briggs stood up, nearly spilling what was left of his coffee. "The damn thing has turned up and you know where it is."

"The trunk has *maybe* turned up," amended Navarro. "And I haven't the vaguest goddamn idea where it is."

Briggs gestured at his bookshelves. "Right after the war—"

"It was 1948."

"In 1948, Coulthard went over to Germany and he located Wisemann's widow someplace or—"

"Munich."

"He found her in Munich and damned if she didn't have a steamer trunk full of Heinrich Wisemann's original drawings. Two hundred and forty-one of them in pen-and-ink, plus letters, pencil sketches and photos. Coulthard had in mind to take the originals and do a series of albums for the American audience. Even back then Wisemann had a pretty fair following in this country. Though nowhere what it is now."

"Not quite what it is now, no. Which is why Coulthard was able to buy the whole shooting match from the Widder Wisemann for five thousand bucks." Navarro poked his finger into the cigarette burn in the sofa cushion next to his. "Experiencing the sort of intellectual orgasm only a dedicated collector can have, Coulthard gathered up his steamer trunk and loaded it on a boat bound for Boston. He traveled on the same damn boat with it, looking after the thing the way you'd look after a sick pet. But — "

"But when he got to America, he hired an independent trucking outfit to haul the stuff to his headquarters somewhere out near Chicago," said Briggs. "The trunk, though, never arrived. It vanished, along with all trace of the truck. Coulthard devoted nearly two years to tracking it, but with absolutely no luck. It's one of the saddest stories in collecting." He took a step toward his friend. "You think the trunk has finally turned up?"

"I'm saying only that three Wisemann drawings that may or may not be from the collection have popped into view."

"Where?"

"Florida. At a comics convention."

"At a comics con? Jesus, I go to those once in a while here in town, and I've never found anything like a Wisemann original."

"Well, *amigo,* at this particular con, on the outskirts of Orlando, Florida, a dealer in paper ephemera sold the three Wisemann originals for five hundred dollars each."

"Boy, why don't I ever walk in on deals like that?"

"Probably because you devote too much of your time to stalking pretty ladies with provocative tits," Navarro suggested. "Be that as it may, an Ajax client got wind of the transaction and he wants us to find the source of those originals. He's hoping they came from the long-lost trunk, and he's willing to pay us to hunt."

"Wait, now. If he knows where the three drawings turned up, why doesn't he just go down to Florida himself and save paying all that money to Ajax?"

"Oddly enough, the notion did occur to him." Navarro glanced toward the windows. "He dispatched a rep down there two weeks ago."

"What did the guy find out?"

"Not one hell of a lot. Due mainly to the fact that he got killed six hours after he stepped off the plane."

"Somebody murdered him?"

"He was hit by a van. If the cops ever find that van they'll probably ask the driver what his intentions were."

After swallowing the last of the coffee, Briggs asked, "You figure there's a possibility we'll get killed, too?"

Navarro shrugged. "I try to keep that sort of thing from happening on any case I work on," he replied. "But there's always the possibility, Jack. Even though I can really use you on this, I'll understand if you don't want to sign on."

"Well, this does sound even riskier than the last one you roped me in on."

"It could well be, *amigo.*"

"Shit, though," said Briggs. "That last one, despite all the trouble, was fun. Three years ago, did you say that was?"

"Three. Doesn't seem that long."

"You know, I'm not in as bad shape as I thought. I did pretty well on those muggers tonight."

"I agree."

"I know more about Wisemann than most anybody."

"Also true."

"And things around here haven't been going especially wonderful. In fact, I have the feeling I'm on the brink of being in the world's biggest slump."

Navarro waited, saying nothing.

"Hell, I'll go," decided Briggs.

5

THE RAVEN-HAIRED FLIGHT attendant smiled down at Navarro, then frowned over at Briggs in the window seat. "Is your friend all right?" she asked Navarro as she leaned closer to him.

There was a folder containing a neat assortment of notes, memos, pictures and photocopies open on Navarro's meal tray. "He was once the sole survivor of an airline crash in the Andes. Ever since, whenever he goes up in a—"

"It's only that he looks so pale and pasty-faced."

"I'm light-complected," put in Briggs, wiping at his perspiring forehead with his handkerchief. "Whenever I sit next to someone who's especially swarthy, the contrast—"

"May I get you a drink?"

"Sure, that sounds...No, nope. I forgot. I don't drink."

"And you, sir?" she asked Navarro.

"Club soda."

She leaned closer, her long, dark hair brushing at his cheek. "With a twist?"

"Lime, thanks."

Smiling, she moved along the aisle.

Briggs said, "Just because rocketing through the sky at twenty thousand feet makes me initially a little uneasy, you don't have to tell people I'm an invalid."

"I was planning to inform her you were a cannibal, but she didn't let me get to—"

"What amazes me is how women—fawn I guess is the word—fawn over you."

"Sincere admiration and recognition of quality isn't technically fawning." He returned his attention to the open folder.

27

"It's too bad you're married and steadfastly loyal, otherwise you could exploit—"

"I'm not married."

Briggs sat up. "Oh, so?" he said. "What happened?"

"We parted."

"When did that—"

"A while ago."

"You could've written, or even phoned. I never exactly, what little I saw of her, much liked Doris. Still, *you* seemed to," said his friend. "You used to look at her with that Disney puppy expression on your poor face and—"

"Let's talk shop." Navarro tapped a photocopy of a police report.

"I always thought you had a stable marriage. Did she leave you, or did you leave her?"

"The former."

Shaking his head, Briggs said, "That's incredible. What reason did she have for—"

"She met someone taller." He passed him a nine-by-twelve photo. "This is Norm Denby."

Briggs took the picture, absently glanced at it. "Ung," he said, turning it over and dropping it to his knee. "How do you get used to looking at pictures of corpses?"

"I don't."

"Was this in that package that came for you express mail to my place this morning?"

"It's a copy of the police file on Denby's death."

"Special delivery and such always makes me uneasy, particularly in the early morning hours." He flipped the photograph face up, shook his head, gave it back. "My creditors favor such means of communication. That and pounding on the door. How come the Orlando cops sent you this confidential stuff?"

"I became acquainted with a very fetching policewoman on a prior visit," he explained.

"I should've deduced that."

Navarro slipped the picture of the dead man back in the file.

"Okay, when our client Kingsmark heard the three Wisemann originals had been sold at the Orlando Comicscon, he sent Denby — a minion at Paradine Pictures who specialized in troubleshooting and top-level gophering — to check the matter out. The photo shows us the end result of that.

"A couple of things struck me in the report. One is that Denby was in a relatively sleazy section of town, one not frequented by tourists. But the site in question is just three blocks from a comics and paper ephemera shop owned and operated by one Mitch Dickerson."

"And he's the guy who sold the Wisemann originals at the convention?"

"The same. The cops didn't know what Denby was up to in Orlando, thus they didn't see anything in the fact that he went on to glory so near the comics joint."

"But was he going there or coming away from the place?"

"That's one of the questions we'll put to Dickerson."

"Because if he talked to Dickerson, then — "

"I tossed in a twist of lemon, too." The attendant smiled at Navarro and set a plastic glass of sparkling water on a clear stretch of his tray. "I take it you're not going to Orlando for Disney World?"

"No, strictly business."

"A shame, since I have a three-day layover there."

"A tragedy," agreed Navarro, grinning with sympathy up at her. "But not to be helped, proving yet again that life is essentially tragic."

"I suppose." She frowned again at Briggs. "Are you really sure, sir, you don't want an aspirin?"

"Bring me a couple. Thanks."

Making a pleased sound, she withdrew.

"With you she wants to frolic for three glorious days and nights," said Briggs. "Me she just wants to keep heavily sedated."

Turning to the second page of the report, Navarro said, "The other thing I noticed was what one of the witnesses to the accident mentioned. He states that 'there was a funny drawing on the side of the van. An orange or something like that with a pair of dark glasses on it.' Suppose the citrus in question was meant to be a lemon?"

"Ah, Blind Lemon, you mean?"

"Seems a possibility. A graphic reference to the late Blind Lemon Jefferson, noted blues singer of the 1920s and sometimes patron saint of folksingers hither and yon. You used to inflict some of his reissue LPs on me when we were roomies long years ago."

"So the driver of the van might be a folk music fan or even a singer himself," said Briggs. "Or maybe he works for some club down there actually called the Blind Lemon."

"Unfortunately, there's not a single bistro with that name in Orlando or environs. I checked," said Navarro. "Keep in mind, too, that the van could be stolen. But even so, the Blind Lemon business may give us a lead and get us to the driver ahead of the cops."

"Too bad nobody got a license number. Then...oh, thanks."

The dark-haired young woman had returned with a cup of water and two aspirin tablets. "Be sure to use the bag there if you really get sick."

"I'll make every effort to," Briggs promised and swallowed the pills. "How are we going to find a van that the police can't locate?"

"By doing any number of shrewd things, *amigo.*" Navarro shut the folder and leaned back.

Navarro closed the bureau drawer on his underwear and carried his empty suitcase to the closet. Stowing it beside his running shoes, he crossed the sand-colored carpeting to the bed and sat down on its edge.

Outside the balcony window, the Florida afternoon was a hazy, glaring blue. The air conditioner was making a low, chill hum.

Navarro flipped open his tan-covered address book, took out a mechanical pencil and slid a complimentary memo pad closer to the phone. Each sheet had *Orlando Rococco Hotel* emblazoned across the bottom, along with some flamingos and a stately palm tree.

He tapped his lower teeth with the eraser end of the pencil, then punched out a number. In less than five minutes and after only three short conversations he reached Detective K.T. McBride.

"I understand the police are looking for a small, compact sex maniac," he said to her, "and I'd like to apply for the job."

"You son of a bitch," she replied.

"Recognized my voice right off, huh?"

"You undersized bastard. Here I risk my law enforcement career by doing you all sorts of favors, and you—"

"Hey, just because an unfortunate genetic defect renders me three inches shorter than you, Kate, is no reason to—"

"*Five* inches shorter, unless you've shot up like a weed since the last time I saw you," she said, angry. "But I'm not pissed off about your diminutive size, Navarro. I'm pissed off about your lying to me."

"Be more specific."

"Tell me how Morris Klass ties in with this alleged hit-and-run you had me pull the file on."

"Oops."

"Yeah, exactly."

Navarro studied his view for a few seconds. "Can flamingos fly?"

"What the hell does that—"

"Thought I just saw a flock of them go flying by me—"

"You know Klass is almost certainly connected, Navarro. So if you have something linking him to that accident, something indicating it was maybe a hit and not—"

"How'd you know I was interested in Klass?"

"Not from anything you told me, you pipsqueak."

"C'mon, Kate, nobody has called a stature-handicapped person a pipsqueak in this country since—"

"You hire, my god, Leo Goldberg's half-assed detective agency to do legwork for you here in Orlando, and yet you don't figure I'm going to find out what that clumsy—"

"Leo's an okay detective," argued Navarro. "Not all that clumsy

31

either, if you've ever seen him on the ballroom floor."

"What do you know about Klass's connection with the death of Norm Denby?"

"*Nada,*" he assured her.

"Then why did you have Leo nosing around in — "

"Kate, you know I've never conned you," he cut in. "If I had even a smidgen of proof that this gang-land kingpin was in any way tied in with — "

"Same old Navarro bullshit."

"It pains me when you cast doubts on my — "

"You're here in town now, right?"

"Freshly arrived."

"I want to see you."

"That's fine, Katie, but keep in mind that I don't think it's wise to rekindle the torrid romance we — "

"I mean I want to see you in a semi-official way," she told him. "Although I hear you and your goofy wife broke up."

Navarro nodded. "You're requesting me to call on you at headquarters?"

"No, not here. Why not have dinner tonight?"

"Being interrogated at meals gives me heartburn."

"I'll be at your hotel at nine. It's the Orlando Rococco, isn't it?"

"The same, but make it ten."

Kate said, "Listen, Rudy, despite the fact that you're an untrustworthy bastard, I do like you."

"Sure, I can tell that. Mostly from the tender way you say bastard, Kate."

"What I mean is, don't go getting yourself killed while you're down here."

"Hey, that's darn good advice. I'll make a note of that."

"See you at ten." She hung up.

Grinning, Navarro made his next call.

6

BRIGGS WENT BACK to his balcony for another look at the view. From his fifth-floor room he could see a pancake house, a seafood-chain place and a souvenir shop on the roadway below. There was also an unobstructed view of another hotel and the outdoor swimming pool of this one.

Frowning, he went and stood again over the bedside telephone. "Rudy'd find out if I used room service," he decided.

Besides which, he'd promised Navarro he wouldn't drink on this trip at all.

"Not that one beer would hurt. Fact is, beer's a proven antidote for jet lag."

He went back to his balcony for another look at the view.

The pool, which looked to be about half Olympic size, sat in the center of a bright green lawn, and there were a dozen or so striped deck chairs arranged on the mosaic tiles bordering it. Two kids were splashing around at the shallow end. Three young women were scattered in the red and white chairs.

"Everybody else must be at Disney World. Or across the way having pancakes."

Briggs avoided the vicinity of the phone this time. He did glance at the bed and wonder how he'd already managed to get it to look unmade.

Tossing his suitcase atop the rumpled bed, he opened it and thrust a hand into the jumble of clothes and paperbacks within. "I packed swim trunks, didn't I? Sure, those floral ones that look like a Rousseau jungle."

He'd neglected to bring a robe, but he found a white terry cloth one dangling in the bathroom. It had *Orlando Rococco* written large across the back.

"And in this corner, the light-heavyweight champion of the world, Orlando Rococco." He started to undress.

By chance, Briggs caught a glimpse of himself in the mirror when he was naked. He concluded that he was pasty-faced from head to foot.

"A tan," he told himself. "That's what I better acquire while I'm down here."

If he got killed — like that poor bastard Denby — he wanted to look good in his casket. That way Ann would realize what a mistake she'd made in abandoning him.

Thinking about Ann made him want a drink again. He fought that temptation, and putting on the robe and trying to conceal as much of his body as possible, he left his room and hurried to the elevators.

"I hate to bother you, but..."

Briggs blinked, but he didn't see anything. Then he recalled he'd stretched out on one of the canvas poolside chairs and covered his face with a copy of *Art Illustrated* he'd found on the deck chair next to his. Apparently he'd drifted off to sleep.

He lowered the magazine. "Yes, ma'am?"

A slim, auburn-haired young woman of about twenty-eight was standing over him. She was very pretty, wearing a one-piece, pale green bathing suit. "Probably I ought just to allow you to go on sleeping," she said, "and retrieve my magazine later. Except I didn't know how long you might — "

"That's okay." He sat up, overcoming an impulse to yawn. "You were doing laps when I sat down. Didn't realize this was yours, although it does seem an odd periodical for a hotel to provide for guests."

"Were you actually reading it, or just using it for a sun shade?" She sat on the footrest of the next chair, knees tight together.

Handing her the copy, Briggs said, "Actually reading it. I'm an artist myself."

"If that'd been a martial-arts magazine, would you be telling me now that you're a guerilla?" She smiled slightly.

Briggs sat up straighter. "Meaning I'm the sort of guy who'd do anything and tell any lie to pick up a pretty woman? Unfortunately, I really am an artist. Well, an art director. So if you don't consider advertising one of the lively arts, maybe I'm not —"

"You know what I've been doing?" Her smile broadened. "Getting back at you for the way the man I sat next to on the flight down here yesterday acted. See, when I told him I'm a high school art teacher in Connecticut, he pretended he —"

"And are you?"

"Oh, yes. I teach at Brimstone High School in...well, obviously in Brimstone, Connecticut."

"A pleasant town. Too expensive for improvident art directors to reside in, though."

"You live, probably, in...um...New York City?"

"On Lexington."

"I've been living with my parents in Brimstone again, since... Do you really want to hear all this?"

"Sure, I'm the avuncular, sympathetic listener sort," he said. "The Phil Donahue of the singles bars."

"I was divorced last year, moved back with my folks for a while."

"I was divorced about two years ago, too."

"That's too bad."

"Not really, no. My name's Jack Briggs, by the way."

"I'm Jenny...Jack Briggs? You're kidding."

"No. If I was going to pretend to be somebody else, I'd pick higher up on the celebrity chain."

"Are you the same Jack Briggs who did covers for Opus Books' science fiction line...oh, about six years ago?"

He grinned. "Eight years ago. I did eleven covers, each and every one of which caused sales on the books they graced to plummet — or, rather, not to rise."

"You're a terrific artist. But how come you quit painting covers? Or are you still and I'm missing them?"

"You never finished giving me your name."

"Oh, sorry. It's Jenny Deacon."

"Pleased to meet you."

"About the covers?"

"The cover painting was a folly of my youth. All over and done."

"That's a terrible shame," Jenny said. "You had a style like nobody else's, and your—"

"I'm an art director now. The pay's a lot better," he said. "Well, it would be were I not between jobs at the moment."

"Are you in Florida looking for work?"

"Nope, just a vacation. Paid for with my severance pay. And you?"

"It's spring vacation at Brimstone High, and I thought I'd enjoy a few days here."

"Alone?"

Jenny nodded. "I don't have too many close friends among my colleagues," she replied. "Did you come down here with anyone?"

Briggs glanced away from her and toward the pool. "I'm with an old school chum of mine."

"A male chum?"

"Sure." He faced her again. "What sort of itinerary do you have, Jenny?"

"A fairly loose one."

"Would you care to have dinner?"

"Tonight?"

"If possible."

"Yes, that would be fine. I'm not—"

"Better clothe yourself, *amigo.*" Navarro had appeared in their midst, wearing denim slacks, a candy-striped shirt and spotless white running shoes.

Briggs frowned. "To what end?"

"We have a meeting to attend."

"So this isn't just a vacation?" said Jenny.

"Jenny Deacon, Rudy Navarro." Briggs slowly and reluctantly got to his feet.

"You're the high point of our excursion thus far, Miss Deacon." Navarro gave her a casual bow. "Forgive me for depriving you of Mr. Briggs's company, but something has—"

36

"I'll meet you at our car in about five minutes," said Briggs.

"Nice to have met you, Miss Deacon." Navarro grinned and took off.

"Is that your old school chum?" Jenny asked.

"That's him," admitted Briggs, watching Navarro go striding off across the bright green grass. "Our meeting shouldn't take that long. Suppose I meet you somewhere at eight?"

"Come by my room, it's 407." She stood, held out her hand. "Call me if something delays you, Jack."

"I won't be delayed." He shook hands with her, then went jogging back toward the peach-colored hotel.

7

AN OLD MAN in shorts, T-shirt and baseball cap was pushing a rattling supermarket cart along the cracked afternoon sidewalk. A single bag of groceries sat in one corner of the metal basket.

Navarro eased the rental Toyota into a parking space. "Denby was hit up near the corner."

Getting out of the passenger seat, Briggs stood watching the retreating old man. "Has it occurred to you, Rudy, that we're on the brink of middle age?"

"Nope." He joined him on the sidewalk.

There were three dry, forlorn palm trees lining this side of the block. The houses were small and faded. The largest was a two-story stucco building the color of pumpkin pie. It had a wide porch covered with a tattered canvas awning, and two old men sat there in canvas-and-tubing rocking chairs. Neither was rocking.

"After middle age," said Briggs as they started walking along, "it's old age, senility and the grave."

"If you live that long."

Briggs shrugged. "But, shucks, why am I downcast? I've just met an ideal woman who—"

"You thought each and every one of your wives was ideal."

"Not ideal in the same way Jenny is."

Halting at the corner, Navarro scanned the intersection and then pointed. "Denby was right about where that oil spot is. The van came from our left, shot around the corner and smacked him."

Briggs looked to their left. "According to the street map, Dickerson's comics shop is down that way."

"Yeah, indicating the van was following him from there—or could've been."

"Denby was coming here to get his car?"

"He'd left it parked across the street, about where that tricycle seems to have expired."

"Why park so far from the store? Walking three blocks through a run-down neighborhood like this at sundown isn't — "

"Maybe he was being cautious."

"Cautious because he suspected somebody was tailing him?"

"*Quién sabe?*" Navarro started walking, turned the corner. "Leo Goldberg says Dickerson's on vacation, but we'll trot over to the shop anyway."

"Flat," commented Briggs as they walked.

"What is?"

"Florida. It's flat, no dimension to it."

They passed a narrow grocery store. A dark-haired young man was sitting on an empty orange crate next to the screen door, playing a guitar that rested across his lap.

"A sad song," Navarro said to him in Spanish.

"Go fuck yourself," the guitarist replied in the same tongue.

"It's great to be bilingual," said Briggs.

The Paper Treasure Shop was on a corner next to a small, dusty old hardware store that looked as though it had opened about the same week indoor plumbing had been introduced to the area. Somebody inside the hardware store was watching a television soap opera, and sounds of passion and accusation drifted out into the glaring afternoon.

Taped on the inside of Dickerson's glass door was a sheet of lined notebook paper with *Away on Buying Trip, back in Few Days* printed on it.

"Interesting coincidence," commented Navarro, "that the one gent who maybe knows where those drawings came from is out of town."

"He's not much of a letterer, mixes up lower case with upper case." Briggs tried the brass doorknob. The door was locked and bolted.

Navarro squatted, shaded his eyes, and looked inside. He poked at the mail slot. "Looks like a couple days' letters and bills piled up on the floor."

Briggs was scanning the display in the window. "Those issues

40

of *Batman* are older than we are. Huh, he's only asking twenty-five for number twenty. Be a good investment, but there must be something wrong with this copy at that price. Nice batch of Big Little Books. *Captain Midnight and the Moon Woman.* Catchy title, wonder what it — "

"You see any Wisemann originals?"

"Nary a one."

Navarro strolled over to the open doorway of the adjacent hardware store. "Excuse me, ma'am, do you happen to know where — "

"Hush," requested a thin, nasal voice. "Wait until the commercials."

Briggs stayed at the comic-shop window. "I used to have that whole run of *Fantastic Four*. Which wife was it who incinerated them?"

"All right, what is it?"

"We're looking for Mitch Dickerson."

"He's away."

"Know where?"

"He and I aren't on intimate terms."

"When's the last time you saw him?"

"Six weeks ago."

"Six weeks? The guy's right next door to — "

"As I explained, we're not on close terms. Truth is, I ... Hush up again. It's back on."

"Thank you." Navarro tipped his imaginary hat and returned to his friend. "Might as well get back to the car."

"In a minute," said Briggs, who was still studying the contents of the window.

The Lakeside Dinner Theatre was actually beside a lake, of which there are many in Orlando. This lake covered about three or four acres, and there was a gray-haired man in a little rowboat out in the middle of it. The parking lot was covered with pink-tinted asphalt, and the high palm trees surrounding it were in excellent health. The theater building was off-white and shaped somewhat like the case an immense piano would be packed in.

"Klass has still got them?" asked Briggs as he stepped out onto the nearly empty parking lot.

"That's what Leo Goldberg reports." Dropping the car keys in his pocket, Navarro stood contemplating the theater-restaurant. "A monument to good taste."

"Is he really tied in with the Mafia?"

Navarro shrugged his left shoulder. "Let's just say he has an unsavory reputation."

"Doesn't sound like the sort of person to buy three Heinrich Wisemann originals."

"Proving once again that life is full of strange and unexpected turns." He walked up to the etched-glass main doors.

A large, plastic marquee was mounted next to the entryway. *Last 3 Perfs. Jerry Marcus and Tiffany St. Joan in "Private Lives."*

When Briggs and Navarro reached the doors, there was a wide, tanned young man on the other side of the glass watching them. He wore white designer jeans, an anonymous gray sweatshirt and dark glasses. Eventually he reached down and pulled the door inward a few inches. "Yes?"

"I'm glad you moved," said Navarro. "For a minute there I thought we'd come to the wax museum by mistake."

"Yes?"

"I'm Navarro, this is Briggs. We have an appointment with Mr. Klass."

"That's right." The big man didn't move.

Navarro grinned at him. "It must be a lot of fun seeing Noel Coward every night."

"Come on in," he invited. "Stop next to the potted palm so I can go over you."

"I left my gun back at the—"

"Don't jiggle." He frisked Navarro, then Briggs. "Okay," he said, but not to them.

They were gathered in the chill, shadowy foyer. Beyond it was an empty, unlit cocktail lounge. Not completely empty, it turned out. Another large man, in his forties and wearing a dark suit, emerged out of the shadows and came toward them, smiling. "I'm Les Janeiro."

"Navarro, also Briggs," explained Navarro.

"If you'll just follow me, gentlemen, I'll escort you to Mr. Klass's office." Crossing the foyer, he moved down a dim corridor. "I'm a great admirer of your work, Mr. Briggs."

"What work?"

"Your cover paintings, of course. I thought the one you did for the second volume in Harlan Ellison's trilogy was brilliant."

"Thanks."

"What caused you to abandon your career?"

"Economic factors."

"It's too bad the days of patrons of the arts are vanished, for the most part." Janeiro stopped at a pale pink door and tapped twice.

The door made a faint whirring sound.

"Go right in, gentlemen." Opening the door, he stood aside.

Briggs entered first and went right over to one of the Wisemann originals. It was about two feet square, in a bamboo-and-acetate frame and hanging on the buff-colored wall at eye level. "Dancing hippos," he said admiringly.

Behind a wide blonde desk sat a lean, dark-haired man of about fifty. His hair was close-cropped but his moustache was large and shaggy. "I'm Morris Klass." He rose.

"Rudy Navarro, and my partner, Jack Briggs."

Klass nodded at Briggs, asking, "You're an admirer of Wisemann's work?"

"Sure. This one was in *Jugend* originally, around 1930 or so. It's never been reprinted."

"Take a look at these, they're even better." The other two framed originals hung side by side on the wall behind Klass's desk. He stood up and moved aside.

Briggs went over to look. "This one of the demons climbing all over the cathedral is great. Never seen it before."

"Nor had I," said Klass.

"The centaur chasing the wood nymph isn't bad," observed

Briggs, "but it's really only a variation on one Wisemann did in 1935 for—"

"It's my favorite."

"Really? Well, I can see where—"

"Are they," put in Navarro, "authentic?"

Briggs turned, nodding. "Certainly, Rudy, sure. There's no doubt about that."

Klass smiled a small smile. "You don't think somebody'd pass off fakes on me, do you?"

"Merely double-checking."

Briggs came around from behind the desk. "A bargain for sure," he said, mostly to himself.

Klass sat down again, gestured at the two chairs facing his desk. "Why's everybody so interested in these three originals?"

Navarro settled into one of the seats. "Somebody besides us?"

Briggs wandered over to examine a framed *Little Nemo* original on another wall.

"The main reason I let you come over for a look," said Klass, "is because I'm curious."

"How many others have shown interest?"

"You're not the only ones."

Navarro leaned forward, resting his palm on his knee. "Was Norm Denby among them?"

"The gentleman who got killed? I never saw him, never met him."

"Talked to him on the phone, huh?"

"Is that what this is about? You think Denby was killed intentionally?"

Navarro shrugged both shoulders. "Too soon to call," he answered amiably. "Who else has been inquiring?"

"Let's just say others," said Klass. "I'm fond of Wisemann, and quite a few other graphic artists and cartoonists. When I heard a few of his drawings had turned up at that comics convention, I went over and bought them. I know his work pretty well, so it's not likely I'd buy a forgery. But now I'm feeling that there's something about these drawings I don't know."

"We all," said Navarro, "have gaps in our knowledge."

"Your Ajax Novelty Company is a top rate and expensive detective agency, despite its cute name," said Klass. "You're supposed to be one of their best men. Briggs I never heard of. Ajax didn't send you here just to talk about a few old cartoons. There has to be more to it than that."

Navarro assumed a guileless look. "You're an affluent collector, we represent another affluent collector," he explained. "He wanted us to take a look at these Wisemann originals, determine that they were genuine. That's where Briggs comes in. Then I'm authorized to make you an offer for — "

"No, forget that. They're not for sale."

"Our client is willing to pay as much as — "

"I'm an affluent collector, as you mentioned, Navarro. The great thing about that is that I never have to sell something I'm fond of."

Briggs came and sat in the other chair. "We're willing to go as high as — "

"Not interested, really." Klass rose out of his chair.

"Perhaps we could contact the dealer you bought them from. Did he have more Wisemanns?"

Klass laughed. "If he did, they'd be on my walls now, too."

"You asked him about his sources?"

"Sure, and got a very vague answer. But most dealers are like that." He inclined his head in the direction of the door.

Navarro and Briggs left the office. In the hallway they were reunited with Janeiro, and he escorted them outside.

As they walked to their car Navarro asked, "You're sure those drawings are real?"

"Absolutely," said Briggs. "But there's no way of telling if they came from the trunk."

8

NAVARRO, ALONE, VENTURED into the editorial floor of the
Orlando *News-Pilot*. The area was silent, and all but one of the
dozen computer terminals was untenanted. Hunched at that one
was a dark-haired young woman of no more than twenty. While
she stared at the greenish display screen and poked at the
keyboard with her middle finger, she puffed at a cigarette, sipped
coffee from a mug with an image of Donald Duck on its side,
and snacked out of a grease-spotted container of french fries.

Sensing Navarro, she glanced up. "It's a terrible habit, I know."

"Which?"

"Smoking." When she gestured with the cigarette hand, ashes
flickered down onto the lap of her jeans. "Oh, and probably junk
food, too."

"The writer's life is not an easy one," he said, wending his way
toward her. "I'm looking for Jiggs O'Hearn."

She made a polite snorting sound. "Isn't that a dumb name?"

"He was probably christened in honor of St. Jiggs, the patron
of—"

"No, it's a nickname, from the character in...oh, you're
kidding. Right?"

"You've found me out. Is O'Hearn in?"

She pointed with the hand that held the coffee. "Back in that
cubbyhole office over there," she told him. "After you open the
door, grasp your nose and stand back for a minute or two. Until
all the foul cigar smoke billows out."

"I'll do that." Grinning at her, he headed for the office. He
knocked on the plywood door.

"Who?" came a throaty voice.

"Navarro."

"Come on in."

Navarro opened the door. The tiny office was indeed thick with bluish smoke.

"See?" called the girl.

After waiting fifteen seconds or so, Navarro ventured across the threshold.

Jiggs O'Hearn was sitting at a desk with a small drawing board lying flat atop it. He had a black cigar in his mouth and was leaning very close to the drawing on the board as he inked it. He was a heavyset man, a few years beyond forty. "Sit where you can," he invited. "I'm behind on my deadline with this one."

Sitting presented a problem, since the political cartoonist occupied the only chair. Navarro moved a stack of back-issue newspapers and took their place on a low, battered filing cabinet. "You're the fellow who alerted Joel Kingsmark to the Wisemann originals.

"Too bad I didn't know about them earlier — would've bought them myself." Squinting, he blacked in the trousers of one of the figures in his drawing. "I really don't feel at home as a political commentator. I'm essentially a bigfoot gag man. Hell, I can't even imitate Ronald Searle like most of my colleagues."

"Who else did you tell?"

"Tell about what?"

"The drawings."

"What makes you think I — "

"Other people have apparently been showing interest."

O'Hearn hunched again. "I never can get the president looking just right. Caricature I have little affinity for," he said. "Kingsmark maybe told you — I'm somewhat of a collector myself. Cartoon buffs are like drug dealers, in that they know all about each other. Know who their rivals are, know who's got what, know when something interesting turns up on the market. At night — I work here instead of at home because my wife...Anyway, I work here and I phone people around the country now and then. Paper pays for it. I keep in touch with collectors that way. When I learned what Klass had picked up, I phoned Kingsmark."

"And who else?"

O'Hearn exhaled smoke. "Well, I know I talked to Rich Collins in Detroit and H.A. MacQuarrie in Frisco. Oh, and to the Webb Gallery in Boston. That's Ethan Webb and his daughter Jennifer. With them, if they get something they want through a tip from me, there's usually a small gratuity, at least there used to be while the old guy was alive. Some political cartoonists win Pulitzers and earn large salaries. I'm not among them."

"Maybe if you learned to draw the president better." Navarro dropped from the cabinet. "Did you see Norm Denby when he came to Orlando?"

"Briefly, yes."

"He was killed near Dickerson's comics shop."

O'Hearn set down his pen. "I know," he said, "and maybe that's my fault. I was the one who told him Dickerson had sold the originals."

"Do you know if Denby actually got to the shop?"

"What do you mean? If he was killed before he saw Dickerson?"

"Yep."

He shook his head, sending a swirl of smoke across the desk. "No, I don't."

"Did you suggest he talk to anyone else?"

"Sure, I told him to see Morris Klass. Klass thinks he's a dedicated collector, but he's just a dabbler," said the cartoonist. "I was fairly certain he'd be willing to sell the Wisemanns."

"Did he actually contact Klass?"

"I don't know."

Navarro asked him, "What do you think the drawings are actually worth?"

"I told Denby to offer Klass fifteen hundred apiece, but they're worth three or four times that."

"Where'd Dickerson get them?"

O'Hearn's laugh segued into a cough. "I couldn't get him to tell me," he said. "It could be somebody simply walked in off the street with the three of them, or he might've picked them up at a flea market for five bucks."

"What'd your guess be?"

"Kingsmark's hoping to locate that missing trunk, isn't he?"

"He'd like to know if that's where they came from."

"It's my theory that either you have luck or you don't." He took up his pen and dipped it in a bottle of india ink. "Me, I've never won a sweepstakes, a lottery, a raffle. Therefore, I have no reason to believe I'll stumble over that trunk full of Wisemann originals."

"Did Dickerson stumble over it, though?"

"I doubt it. Because if he had any other Wisemanns, now that other people are interested, he'd have pulled out a few more to sell."

Navarro asked, "Do you know where Dickerson is?"

"He should be at that run-down shop of his."

"He hasn't been. The only listing for him in the phone book is the shop. Does he live in some other town?"

"My impression is he sleeps on a cot in the back room and cooks his meals on a hot-plate there," he said. "At least the place sure smells like it."

"Is he likely to phone you?"

"No, I don't deal with him much. He usually doesn't get in many originals." The cartoonist took the cigar out of his mouth, snuffed it out in a seashell ashtray. "This whole business, you know, doesn't make much sense."

"Amplify."

"Well, you obviously think Denby was killed on purpose," O'Hearn said. "Now, collectors can be mean-minded and selfish at times, but, hell, Navarro, nobody'd kill anyone over a few drawings."

"Not a few, no," he agreed.

The jukebox was expressing great sadness at the top of its

voice. The walls of the narrow, smoky restaurant seemed to be shaking, but that may have been caused by the noise and motion of the crowd of patrons in Shark Egan's Cafe and not by the mournful country-and-western music cascading out of the machine.

"*Caramba*," observed Navarro.

"This isn't LA," reminded K.T. McBride.

"I began to suspect that soon after we arrived."

"The seafood here is absolutely the best in this whole damn part of Florida."

"That's nice to know. I thought maybe people just came here because they weren't allowed to wail and stomp at home."

"The thing to do is relax," advised the blonde policewoman. She picked up the one-page photocopied menu.

A broad-shouldered young man in plaid shirt, Levi's and a straw sombrero went striding by their booth, apparently practicing his hog calling.

Kate rested her elbows on the raw wood table. "What did you find out from Klass?"

"Eh?" Navarro cupped a hand to his ear.

"I want to know how he's involved with this hit-and-run."

"He isn't." Navarro rested his elbows on the raw wood table. "I happen to believe, K.T., that beneath that facade that would give prison matrons the heebiejeebies you are a sweet, decent girl — just the sort that Louisa Mae Alcott, were she still above the sod, would celebrate in uplifting prose. Therefore I am going to confide in you every single detail of this case, even things I've vowed never to tell to a living soul."

"You've lived too close to Hollywood for too long. You're as full of crap as an agent."

"More so, actually, according to recent lab tests."

"Damn it, Navarro, if Denby was murdered I want —"

"Far as I know, hon, he —"

"God, I hate to be addressed as 'hon.'"

"I know, I remembered." He grinned. "The first rule of

Mexican kung fu is to get one's opponent off balance. As I was saying, I have no reason to believe Denby's shuffling off wasn't due to a vehicular misfortune."

"Why see Klass, then?"

"My client — or rather the client of the monolithic organization I work for — collects drawings."

"Drawings of what?"

"The subject matter isn't important, Kate. It's who done it," he explained. "In this instance the artist in question is a fellow named Heinrich Wisemann."

"I've seen his stuff in a paperback collection my former husband had."

"Couple of weeks ago three original drawings by Wisemann, worth between twenty and thirty thousand dollars, turned up here in your tropical hometown. Denby worked for our client and was sent —"

"How much longer are you going to take to make up your god-damn minds?" A large, shaggy waiter in T-shirt, dungarees and tattered white apron loomed beside their booth and tapped at his order book with a stub of yellow pencil.

Kate said, "I'll have the shrimp Creole."

"What about you, shorty?"

"That time of the month for you, huh?" said Navarro, scanning the menu. "Bring me the swordfish steak."

"Was that a snotty remark?"

"The farthest thing from."

"Okay, then." The waiter scribbled on the pad and left.

"Somebody's going to poke you eventually," Kate said.

"Several already have, yet that hasn't dampened my good humor."

"So Denby came here to buy these drawings?"

"That's it, yes, Kate. Klass had them and —"

"Denby was in contact with Klass, then?"

"Klass says they never met."

"But he could be lying. Maybe he and his associates arranged that accident."

"For why?"

She thought a few seconds. "Are the drawings worth a lot more than you think?"

"Nope."

"Klass and Denby might've gotten into a fight over them."

"Unlikely."

Kate sighed. "But, Navarro, this all must fit together."

"We don't have enough pieces, yet, and we aren't even sure what it is we're building."

"True, but—"

"Enough shoptalk," he suggested. "Let's yell about something else."

Navarro was finishing his fifth phone call when a knock sounded on the door of his room.

He hung up, bounced off his bed and approached the door. "*Sí?*"

"Alone in there?"

"To the best of my knowledge." He unlocked the door and tugged it open. "Come in, *amigo*. My hotel room is your hotel room, as my people say."

Briggs entered, smiling. "I realize I've only known Jenny for—"

"Whoa," advised Navarro as he shut the door. "Is this going to be another true confession?"

Briggs went and sat in the room's armchair. "Did you ever wonder how many imitation Utrillos there are in the hotel and motel rooms of America?"

"Nope, never." He settled again on the edge of his bed. "If you're planning to give me a detailed account of your conquest of the schoolmarm, let's postpone it until tomorrow. The midnight hour's been here and gone."

"I'll listen to an account of your adventures with the world's tallest policewoman first if you want. Since I'm in such a tiptop mood."

"I have no such report to pass along. For tonight I've been concentrating on duty," said Navarro. "I don't know if you've

53

heard about the grasshopper and the ant. It was in all the papers and *60 Minutes* gave it eight minutes. The moral of that — "

"Hey, I looked at the damn originals. Told you they're legit." Briggs frowned. "You said you didn't need me along on your other excursions tonight."

"Where'd you take Jenny?"

Briggs studied the carpeting near his feet. "This was her idea, actually, and I never thought I'd do something like this," he said. "We went to Disney World. You can catch a shuttle right in front of our hotel."

"You can catch a shuttle at just about any given spot in Orlando."

"I really enjoyed myself." Briggs took a deep breath, smiling. "You have to keep in mind that I haven't enjoyed myself much in quite some time. Certainly not while sober."

"You're sticking with the sobriety?"

"It's two days now. Haven't had a drink since that night in Alfie's Pub."

"That's good."

"I'm going to stick with it."

"Don't link it with Jenny Deacon."

"She's really a splendid woman, Rudy," Briggs said. "It's odd, too, because I usually tend to be fascinated by bitchy types. Ann being a good example. Jenny, though, is very different. She's amiable, supportive, bright..."

"Thrifty, reverent and brave." Navarro yawned. "This romance has lasted longer than many. Since well before noon."

"Okay, I know I sometimes get overly enthusiastic about a new woman."

"Marsha Marie Quinlan."

Briggs said, "Jesus, Rudy, that was in our Junior year. You thought she was great, too. You used to ogle her like a wolf in a Tex Avery cartoon."

"Chevrolet."

"All right, she did borrow my car to go spend a weekend in Carmel with that jock from the Deke house."

54

"A week. She and your sole means of transport were gone a solid week."

"I'm older now, possibly even more mature. My judgment has improved."

"Just keep in mind, *amigo*," said Navarro, "that we're on a job. Not a nine-to-five situation, but a job that may involve people who run down other people in the street and kill them. Be romantic, but be damn careful, too."

"You're commencing to sound like a public service announcement for preventing AIDS." Briggs got up. "I take it you weren't successful with K.T. the cop? That would explain why you're so sour about my fun-filled evening with Mickey Mouse and the gang."

"*Adiós*," said Navarro.

"Okay, I'll see you for breakfast." Briggs walked to the door. "About nine?"

"Eight."

"Good night." He left.

Navarro picked up the phone.

9

BRIGGS HAD BETTER luck in Kissimmee. He located the town's comics shop at a few minutes beyond two in the afternoon. Had he not gotten tangled up on the highways from Orlando he'd have made the twenty-mile drive in at least a half hour less than he did. This was the fourth such establishment he'd hit since parting from Navarro after breakfast. He'd found out nothing thus far.

The narrow sign proclaimed *Comicman's*. The place was wedged between a dingy laundromat and a shop that had gone broke trying to sell popcorn in ninety-nine different flavors.

Adopting his most pleasant demeanor, Briggs entered. Actually, he wasn't feeling that bad. He was in love, and he didn't have a hangover.

"Freddie isn't here." Behind the counter lurked an enormous dark-haired woman wearing a paisley mother hubbard. She was wedged in a white wicker chair, reading a copy of a motorcycle magazine.

"Then perhaps you can help me."

There was just enough room on the glass counter to rest an elbow. Doing that, Briggs took out a photocopy from his shirt pocket. He was careful not to topple the plastic-bagged stacks of recent Marvel titles or nudge the cartons of gum cards.

"Freddie's the only one who can buy or trade."

Unfolding one of the copies of a Wisemann drawing he'd made at the Orlando public library that morning, Briggs held it toward the huge woman. "Actually, ma'am, I'm interested in knowing if anyone's been in lately offering to sell you—"

"Freddie doesn't buy originals."

"Even so. Has anyone tried to sell you drawings by this particular artist?"

"I can't tell one of these assholes from another."

"But Wisemann has a distinctive style."

"Wait a minute." Folding down a corner of the magazine page, she dropped it to her lap and held out a pudgy hand. She had rings on three of the available fingers. "I only see good close up."

He handed her the copy, then glanced around the shop. There were five rickety tables loaded with boxes of old comic books. "Nice little establishment you have here."

"You ought to see the assholes who come in to buy this crap." She brought the drawing up close to her face. "Wisemann. I remember the name."

"From somebody who tried to sell —"

"Sure, that's right. One of them had these same kind of dancing hippos. Wasn't the same picture, but sort of like it."

"Who brought them in?"

Sighing, she closed her eyes. "I try not to look most of these assholes in the face, since I have a delicate stomach. Let me see if I can conjure up an image."

"When was this?"

"Hold on, I'm still trying to remember what he looked like."

"He? It was a man?"

"Women have more sense than to come into a dump like this." She opened her eyes. "A hippie."

"A hippie?"

"Long, blond hair down to here. Ratty clothes. Haven't you heard of hippies?"

"Not in almost a decade."

"Skinny guy, twenty-five or thirty. Pale. Probably a pothead."

"Did he give you a name?"

After closing her eyes for nearly a minute, she opened them. "No, because Freddie doesn't buy originals."

"When was this?"

"Seems to me it must've been three, four weeks ago."

"The guy ever been in before?"

58

"Not while I've been here."

"Since?"

"Naw."

"He mention where he lived?"

"We never got into much of a conversation. I just happen to remember the name Wisemann and those cute hippos."

Nodding, Briggs started to turn away. Then he stopped, asking the fat woman, "How many originals did he have for sale?"

"Five."

"Five?"

"Working in this hole hasn't turned my brains to mush," she informed him. She held up her right hand, fingers spread out. "I can still count. Five."

"So there *are* more," he muttered.

"What?"

"If that fellow comes in again..." Briggs lettered his name and the hotel phone number on the back of the copy of the Wisemann drawing. "Have him phone me."

"You collect this kind of crap?"

"Yes, I do."

"I'll tell Freddie. That way we can buy the drawings and then resell them to you at a stiff markup."

"Well, the thing is, I'm anxious to talk to this fellow with the drawings. If you can arrange that, I'll pay you and Freddie a fee."

"What size fee?"

"Fifty bucks."

"A hundred."

"Okay."

"We're saving up to buy me a new Harley."

Grinning at her, he headed for the door. "Good luck to you."

"I need it, tied up with an asshole like Freddie."

Outside on the hot afternoon street Briggs gave a hopeful laugh. "Maybe there is a trunk hereabouts someplace."

Navarro didn't look up from the yellow legal tablet he was

writing on. "Any progress?"

"Some. And you?" Briggs dropped into the poolside deck chair next to him.

"Tell me what you got first." Navarro leaned back, capping his pen.

"There are more Wisemann originals than the three Klass got."

"How many more?"

"At least two."

"Still shy of a trunkload."

"I'm optimistic, nonetheless," said Briggs and filled his partner in on what he'd found out in Kissimmee.

Navarro said, "That visit was probably paid before he sold the batch to Dickerson."

"Might be. You figure he hasn't tried to unload any since Denby got killed?"

"Not sure." Navarro tapped the top page of his tablet. "I've been tracking down the competition, the rival collectors Jiggs O'Hearn alerted."

"And?"

"From what I've been able to find out, none of 'em was in Orlando at the time Denby was knocked off, with the exception of Klass."

"How about their whereabouts now?"

"Richard Collins remains at home in Detroit," answered Navarro. "H.A. MacQuarrie of Frisco checked into one of the hotels over at Disney World yesterday. The Webb Gallery of Beantown has been shut up tight for a week, and nobody knows where Papa Webb or his distaff offspring are."

"Seems to be a lot of that going around."

"I dropped by Dickerson's shop again this afternoon."

"How'd you accomplish that? I had the car."

"K.T. gave me a lift."

"That fits the pattern."

"What pattern?"

"All upwardly mobile Latins lust after tall blondes."

"Lust is not one of the words that can be correctly used to

describe my feelings about Kate. Anyway, the mail wasn't there."

"On the other side of his door?"

"That mail, yes. Meaning that Dickerson, or someone near and dear to him, has been sneaking in to gather it up."

"So he's not out of town. He's lying low someplace, popping into the shop now and then."

"But why the hell is he hiding at all?"

"Probably afraid of being felled by a van," suggested Briggs. "Have you found out anything about the Blind Lemon, by the way?"

"*Nada.*" Navarro scratched at his curly hair with his pen. "Now, Jack, what kind of message can we leave for Dickerson that'll smoke the nitwit out?"

"Comics."

"Hum?"

"We tell him we've got a load of rare comic books that we want to sell cheap. We're in a hurry, so he's got to act quick."

"Hey, that's good." Navarro sat up, rubbing his hands together. "Yeah. I'm an old widow living in a mobile-home park near here. My idiot husband just kicked off and I'm stuck with a couple of immense boxes of old comic books from the 1930s and 1940s. I think it's all garbage, but I know this sort of stuff is valuable and I have to get at least five dollars apiece. I have to bury the old coot, and if Dickerson's not fast in replying I'll have to sell to some other dealer." He bounced twice on the canvas chair. "We'll concoct a list of magazines that are worth a bloody fortune and give him a phone number at a mobile-home setup where I happen to know the manager."

"Matter of fact, I picked up the latest comic book price guide during my travels this afternoon," said Briggs. "We'll use that to make sure we get the right kind of bait."

"Good, excellent."

"Who's going to impersonate the widow?"

"We'll flip a coin."

10

THE NEXT EVENING it rained, and Briggs broke his vow.

He took Jenny Deacon to dinner at a French restaurant that looked as though it had been transplanted from New Orleans. Briggs had never been to New Orleans, but he'd seen it in several movies. Their table was near a narrow window that looked out on a walled courtyard, and there were wrought-iron bars guarding the glass. The wall lamps were also of wrought-iron, and there was considerable red plush and dark wood paneling all around.

The fountain out in the rainy courtyard was topped by a bronze nymph clutching a dolphin. The dolphin didn't look too happy and he was spewing out a stream of water. The night rain hit at them and splashed off their blue-streaked exteriors and into the overfull fountain.

"I'm sorry I even suggested it," Jenny was saying. She wore a black cocktail dress and looked absolutely terrific. "It hadn't occurred to me that —"

"I sort of promised myself I'd refrain."

She said, "It's just that you seem in an especially cheerful mood tonight, Jack. I don't know why that is exactly, but it seemed to suggest you might have a reason for celebrating. Which is why I suggested champagne."

"Don't get the idea I'm an alcoholic," he said. "I don't go on incredible binges if I drink a glass of champagne."

"I know, you want to quit drinking for a while." She picked up her large, gilt-covered menu. "My father was a very heavy drinker, and he went through some incredible struggles trying to cut down."

"Hey, I'm not struggling," Briggs assured her. "They didn't just release me from Bellevue with a stern warning to drink no more."

"I'm studying the menu," she said, smiling. "I've completely forgotten I made the suggestion about the champagne." Lowering the menu, she looked directly across the small, round table at him. "You are happy about something, though, aren't you?"

"Besides being with you? Well, yes, as a matter of fact."

"Is it something you can tell me about?"

Briggs shook his head. "Not exactly."

"Don't tell me I'm dating a secret agent."

"Nope, I'm not a spy. Not a drug runner, either." He lifted up his menu and opened it wide. "The situation is, I'm not just down here on a vacation, Jenny."

"You don't owe me any explanations," she said. "Meeting at a hotel in Florida is pretty much like meeting on a cruise ship."

He caught the attention of their gaunt waiter. The man's crisp, red jacket crackled as he bowed. "Sir?"

"A bottle of Moët."

Jenny said, "Jack, you really don't have — "

"Hush."

Bowing again, the waiter departed.

"You really shouldn't drink if you — "

"We're celebrating, remember?"

"All right, but you're making me feel as though — "

"The whole thing is starting to sound much more serious than it really is," he said.

The rain hit hard at the window of Jenny's room.

"And you're a detective, too?" she asked.

Briggs drank some of the champagne in his plastic room-service wine glass. "Navarro's a full-fledged detective," he explained, leaning forward on the sofa. "I'm really what I told you I was. See, I'm being entirely honest with you. That's because this isn't just a shipboard romance, Jenny. Navarro is an investigator with a detective agency called the Ajax Novelty Company out in Los Angeles. He's really a hell of a good

64

detective, and we've known each other since college. I already told you that."

She was sitting in the armchair, shoes off, long legs tucked under her. "You still haven't gotten around to telling me why you're especially happy today."

"Ah, you're absolutely right." He refilled his glass. "More?"

"Not just yet, thanks."

"Well, we're looking, as I told you, for the Wisemann originals."

"That's very exciting," she said. "I remember the first time I saw some of Wisemann's sketches reprinted. He was a marvelous graphic artist."

"Right, and each one's worth several thousand." He drank some champagne. "This Chateau Orlando brand isn't that bad. Not Moët, but okay."

Jenny smiled.

"Anyway, we've been trying to track down this Dickerson guy."

"He's which? The one who owns the comics shop and sold the drawings?"

"That's him. He's been lying low and generally unavailable. Rudy got the notion — that's Navarro. Navarro noticed that Dickerson's mail was being picked up. So we concocted a fake letter and slipped it through the mail slot in the shop door. We told him we had all these old comic books — *Action* #15, *Marvel Mystery* #20, *Whiz* #5 — a whole batch of stuff like that. Listed all the titles. I wrote the letter. Used a sheet of lavender note paper with apple-blossom borders. I affected a dainty hand. I'm the widow, and my husband had all this crap, and I heard someplace that comic books like this were worth money, but it's all garbage to me. So I'm going to get rid of them now he's kicked off. I want $500, though, because I know this junk is valuable to collectors. Thing is, I must absolutely have the money right away. Or I'll go to another dealer I heard of about forty miles from here."

"How much would these mythical magazines really be worth?"

"At least $20,000."

Jenny laughed. "That drew him out of hiding, I imagine."

"Surely did, yes ma'am. Dickerson phoned the number we put on the note. It's the manager's office at a mobile-home park where Navarro is well known. Dickerson was disappointed that the widow wasn't in, but he left a message and his phone number. Her name, by the way, is Mrs. Marie A. Novsam."

"A nice name."

"Novsam was my dentist in Manhattan, until we came to disagree about how much one had to pay for a crown. I had an aunt named Marie. Did I mention that? The Marie came from her. Plump lady, walked with a decided limp. Thought I had great promise, but died before she was proven wrong. Anyway, Navarro, posing as Mrs. Novsam's nephew, phoned Dickerson and set up an appointment to bring the comic books to where he's hiding out. Tomorrow morning at eleven-thirty."

"That's wonderful. He's still right here in Orlando?"

Briggs finished the champagne in his plastic glass and refilled. "Not exactly."

"Do you think Dickerson has the trunk?"

"We think he maybe knows who does."

She pressed her palms together. "It will be a very important find."

"Not as impressive as Tut's tomb, but not bad, either."

She stood up. "If you're not a detective, what are you? You still haven't told me."

"Boy wonder."

"What's that?"

"You know, Navarro is Batman. I'm Robin the Boy Wonder."

She came over, joined him on the sofa. "I don't especially like the painting on the wall up there."

"Fake Utrillo," he said, and kissed her.

11

BRIGGS AWOKE FROM a sci-fi dream, one involving sizzling death rays and an alien plot to barbecue him. There was a strip of bright sunlight intruding through the gap in the drapes and striking his slightly puffy morning face.

The bed seemed unusually hard. Opening his eyes he discovered he was on the floor and had apparently been sleeping there.

"My lord, what a morning." He yawned, gulped in air, blinked. "Still, this is far from being the world's worst hangover."

He grunted, groaned, and got himself in a sitting-up position. In fact, he felt only moderately awful. The whanging deep inside his skull was well below the intolerable level, and his mouth felt only moderately flocked.

Now, to apologize to Jenny for falling out of her bed. Most etiquette books don't cover such situations. What to say to one's hostess upon being discovered on the floor beside her bed recovering from a drunken stupor?

Craning his neck, he looked over at the bed. It was neatly made, unrumpled and undisturbed. Nobody was in it or on it.

"Jenny?" Briggs managed to rise up.

Then he noticed his suitcase lying open on the floor nearby. Rotating his head carefully, he scanned the hotel room.

It was not Jenny's, it was his.

Sometime during the night he must've made his way back here.

"Another definite social blunder."

Briggs discovered he was fully clothed and wearing his shoes. So at least he'd dressed before taking his leave of Jenny and stumbling home.

"Oy," he observed, sitting gingerly on the neat bed and reaching for the phone.

After concentrating for less than a minute, he recalled her room number and punched it out. He let the thing ring eight times, then hung up. His wristwatch indicated the time was a few minutes beyond nine. She was probably out at breakfast.

"Did she throw me out last night?"

No, he would've remembered that.

Briggs had to meet Navarro in less than an hour. He headed into the bathroom, undressed, and turned on the shower.

The water that came bursting out of the shower head was icy. Briggs shifted from foot to foot outside the stall, testing the temperature with his hand. Eventually the water became tepid and he stepped under it.

"I'm really an asshole," he said aloud as he used the complimentary shampoo. "Promised Rudy I wouldn't touch booze for the duration of this job and then...Well, hell, it was only champagne."

He hadn't switched to scotch later, had he?

No, he was fairly certain he'd stuck with champagne.

"Still, you were stupid. You don't have any control of yourself. Jesus, you can only vaguely remember what it was like making love to Jenny. No wonder a whole flock of wives dumped you."

Turning his back to the shower head, he soaped his crotch. He sang a few lines from one of Blind Lemon Jefferson's blues.

"Oh, there's one kind favor I ask of you. One kind favor I ask of you. Please see that my grave is kept clean," he boomed. "Dig my grave with a silver—Yikes!"

He grabbed the shower curtain open.

Navarro was standing there, holding up a sheet of hotel paper.

"What are we playing?" inquired Briggs. "Remake of *Psycho*?"

Navarro tapped the message he'd printed on the piece of salmon-hued paper.

Don't talk!

"Huh?"

Making a hushing gesture with finger to his lips, Navarro

backed away from the stall and then out of the bathroom.

Briggs shrugged and turned off the water. After drying himself off with a shaggy hotel towel, he put back on all the clothes he'd shed. Out in the bedroom, Navarro was on hands and knees. He looked under the bed, then beneath the desk and the coffee table.

Nodding, puzzled, Briggs returned to the bathroom and attempted to shave without looking at himself too closely in the mirror. When he was finished, he returned to his partner.

"It's okay to babble now." Navarro held up a small electronic bugging device. "Found this behind the imitation Utrillo and incapacitated it."

"What made you hunt for it?"

"Found a similar device in my room this morning."

"How'd you come to suspect there was a bug in your room?"

"A hunch."

"Art collectors are getting damn sophisticated."

"Two million dollars always brings out the best in people." Navarro sidehanded a scatter of magazines and newspapers off the armchair and sat. "How was your evening on the town?"

"Fine," answered Briggs. "We don't know how long those bugs have been in place, so the opposition may—"

"I don't believe much harm's been done, *amigo*. I did all my dealing with Dickerson and the mobile-home enclave over pay phones while I was roaming this fair, sun-drenched metropolis." Navarro tossed up the disabled bug and caught it. "Far as I can recollect, we haven't discussed much of great moment whilst actually in either of our rooms."

"I guess that's so, yeah."

"Therefore, only you and I are aware that we've located the elusive Dickerson."

Briggs returned again to the bathroom and picked up his hairbrush. "That's true," he agreed.

"This is our exit coming up." Navarro was slouched in the passenger seat. "Sunville."

"Splendid name for a town." Briggs guided their car into the right-hand lane. "A possible place to spend my declining years," he said, "which started about last Tuesday, I think."

They left the highway, curved around the exit ramp and came out on a street lined with car lots and pottery stands. There was a stretch of grassland on the other side of the road and a single tan jackrabbit bounding along it.

"You haven't," mentioned Navarro, "regaled me with an account of your adventures of last night."

"I haven't, no."

"Did things go awry?"

"I don't think so."

Navarro scrutinized a row of plaster dwarves lined up in front of a souvenir shop they were passing. "Four Grumpys and not a single Doc."

Briggs said, "I'm possibly in the midst of a crisis."

"Because of Jenny?"

"No, it's...Shit, Rudy, I didn't keep my word."

"About what?"

"Not drinking while we're down here."

"Is that what this hangdog stuff is all about?"

"I wasn't going to tell you about it."

"Jack, I know you got drunk last night."

"How'd you figure that out?"

"Because you always sleep on the floor when you come home drunk in the middle of the night. At least you used to."

"I could've slept on the bed, then made it up."

"Naw." Navarro laughed. "You don't even know how to make a bed. Even if you did, you wouldn't have done it before taking a shower."

"Actually, the past few years I've been passing out atop my bed. I must be regressing, probably because I'm teamed with you again."

"Pecans," Navarro read off a store sign. "Imagine devoting your entire life to vending pecans."

70

"It was only champagne. We went to this French place, Chez Tardi, and champagne seemed appropriate."

"Your idea?"

"More or less. Well, Jenny suggested it first," said Briggs. "See, she doesn't know about my drinking problem."

"Oh, do you have one of those?"

Briggs drummed his fingers on the steering wheel. "Yeah, I do," he said finally. "But last night I was trying to convince everybody that I don't."

"Takes a while to kill some habits."

"I'm going to quit, Rudy."

"Okay."

"You don't believe me."

"I wouldn't believe you belonged to the Christmas Club until you'd made a few payments."

"Yeah, that's right. Being sober for a few days doesn't set the world's record for sobriety."

"Give it another try."

"The problem is — well, I don't want to miss anything. That includes drinking."

"You haven't missed much. And you're way ahead in some areas, like hangovers and wives," said Navarro. "This is our street coming up on the right."

12

THE DOG STARTED to bark before they were even out of the car — a big, black dog, chained to the trunk of the lone orange tree in the weedy front yard. The few oranges dangling on the branches were pale green and splotched, the hurricane fence around the small yard was rusted and sagging.

"Heavier," said Briggs, stopping on the cracked sidewalk to survey the small white cottage where Dickerson was holed up.

"What?" Navarro had lifted a cardboard box out of the back seat of their crimson Toyota.

"That box is supposed to hold a hundred old comic books. Act like it's heavier."

"Are you claiming a hundred funny books weigh more than two phone books, three days of the Orlando *News-Pilot* and a Gideon Bible?"

"Old comic books had more pages." Briggs pushed the sprung-wire gate open.

The black dog, hair standing on end along its spine, barked and protested.

"Nice pup." Navarro was hefting the box and walking with his legs slightly bowed.

"Not that heavy," advised Briggs.

The lower frame of the screen door was missing its screen, and the wooden door behind it had peeling paint. Briggs thumbed the doorbell, but the ring didn't produce any action within the small, ramshackle house. Down on the railroad tracks a block away a freight train went rumbling by.

The dog had stopped barking. It was snarling now, struggling mightily to break its chain and get at them.

Navarro set the box down, yanked the screen door open and booted the wooden door several times. "Hey, Dickerson, we're anxious to sell these damn comics."

The door opened a few inches. A tall, balding man of about thirty squinted at them. "Identify yourselves."

"We're the guys with the comic books."

Picking up the box, Navarro kicked the door again and then nudged his way inside. Briggs followed. The balding man had been propelled back against a fat purple sofa.

"What the fuck are you guys—"

"Sit down," suggested Navarro, "and we'll chat."

"No, you get the hell out of here. I'm not going to do business with—"

"But we're eager to do business with you." Dropping the box to the floor, Navarro sat in a fat orange armchair. "That is, if you're Dickerson."

"Of course I am." He eyed the box. "All right, I guess I can take a look."

"You've probably already seen the local phone directories," said Navarro.

"Huh?"

"Sit," invited Briggs, nodding at the sofa.

"I've been expecting this," said the comics dealer as he sat, reluctantly. "Randy sent you, huh?"

Briggs went over to stand in the doorway to the next room. "Who's Randy?"

Dickerson rubbed at his nearly hairless head. "Mind if I smoke?"

"This isn't an airplane, go ahead." Navarro leaned forward in the chair. "You can start by explaining who Randy is and why you're hiding."

Dickerson took a pack of filtered cigarettes out of the pocket of his Hawaiian shirt. He shook one out and lit it with a wooden match. He coughed.

"First, suppose you fuckers tell me who you are."

"I'm Navarro, he's Briggs."

"What's that mean? I want to know why you bastards come shoving into my place here."

"We're with a private detective agency." Navarro lifted his right buttock, slid out his wallet. "Here you see a copy of my credentials." He held up his open wallet.

"Just a minute." Dickerson picked up a pair of rimless glasses off the coffee table, put them on and got up. He came over to look. "LA, huh?"

"The glamour capital of the world, yes."

"Why are you here?"

"The Wisemann originals," said Briggs.

"Randy again." Dickerson went back and sat down. "His wife's family hired you, right?"

Navarro asked, "Why would they do that?"

Dickerson remembered his cigarette and took a puff. "Okay, if you're not from them, then what the fuck do you want with me?"

"We'll take this in easy stages," said Navarro, leaning back. "And if you're helpful the agency will provide an honorarium."

"How much is that in dollars?"

"Fifty."

"A hundred would be better."

"It surely would," agreed Navarro, smiling pleasantly. "But fifty is what we're paying."

"Do I get it now, in front?"

"Talk some, first."

"About what?"

"Commence by telling us who Randy is."

Dickerson coughed. "You guys really don't know? Well, I'm not sure what the fuck his name is. He calls himself Randy Sunn. That's his, you know, professional name."

"What's his profession?"

"Right now he's a deadbeat," answered the dealer. "He used to be, from what he told me, some kind of folksinger. That was out in San Francisco. He even tried to run his own club, out in the Mission District someplace."

"The Blind Lemon," provided Briggs.

Dickerson looked over at him. "Yeah, that's right. But if you know that, how—"

"The Wisemann originals that you sold at the con," cut in Navarro. "They belonged to Randy Sunn?"

"In a way, sure. What I mean is, Randy sold them to me." He shook his head. "Shit, you know, I shouldn't've messed with them at all."

"They were stolen?"

Dickerson snuffed out his cigarette in a crowded green glass ashtray. "That sort of depends on how you look at it."

Navarro said, "Explain."

"Okay, well, Randy was married. Maybe not exactly married, but he was living with this girl in her family's place in Marin County. You know where Marin is, right across the Golden Gate Bridge from San—"

"We know. Continue."

"It was a big old house there in Marin, in San Rafael I think. When he and this girl broke up—his wife or whatever she was—Randy, he, you know, borrowed some of the stuff that belonged to her and her family. There was, though I never saw it, some jewelry and some rare books. There was also a big trunk, according to Randy, full of drawings."

"Bingo," observed Briggs.

"Why'd he take the trunk?" asked Navarro. "Must've been heavy. Jewels and books are a lot easier to carry."

"Randy had the idea the drawings were valuable—maybe from something his wife told him. I don't know. He liked some of them, too, so he decided to take the whole damn trunk."

"Have you seen the trunk itself?" asked Briggs.

Dickerson shook his head. "No, only a half-dozen or so of the Wisemann drawings. Randy told me about the trunk, though."

"A half dozen?" said Navarro.

"That's what he brought in to have me try and sell. But I took just three. You know, I wasn't sure I could unload even those. But the way other people showed such an interest..." He trailed off and lit a new cigarette.

"Was Norm Denby one of the people?"

"Who?"

"The chap who got killed almost in front of your shop."

Dickerson looked everywhere but at them. "Listen, that wasn't supposed to happen."

"What *was* supposed to happen?"

"That's why I haven't been going into my shop much and been staying here at my buddy's place while he's out of town."

"Randy killed him, didn't he?"

"Well, yes, but that wasn't what he intended at all." Dickerson puffed at his cigarette, coughing again. "Denby phoned me and said he was interested in Wisemann originals, especially in a whole trunk full of them. He made an appointment to come and talk to me at my shop. Okay, so I got in touch with Randy. But he was sort of paranoid about this, he didn't see it as a chance to make money at all. He figured Denby was probably some kind of detective hired by his wife or her family to track him down."

"Do you know the young lady's name?" asked Briggs.

"Emily, I think."

"The family's name?"

"It was an odd name. Something like Coldheart. Could that be a real name?"

"Close enough." Navarro stood. "How'd Randy come to kill Norm Denby?"

"Instead of, see, meeting with him directly, Randy hunkered down in my back room and just listened while Denby and I talked." Dickerson shook his head again. "To me the guy sounded legit. You run into people like that sometimes, somebody working as a go-between for a rich collector. So it didn't surprise me that Denby didn't know all that much about Wisemann."

"Randy didn't agree with your judgment?"

"No, he didn't. Because Denby didn't know much about originals or Wisemann and because he was from California. LA's six hundred miles from Frisco, but that didn't convince Randy. He was certain Denby was really a private cop sent to nab him. So anyway, Denby leaves, saying he'll check back with me that night. Then Randy — Jesus, this is stupid — Randy follows him in his van. What he claims he wanted to do was just sideswipe the guy, maybe give him a broken leg or a couple cracked ribs — something that would incapacitate him while Randy got his stuff gathered up and took off."

"He told you all that?"

"Not before, but afterwards."

"Instead of hobbling Denby, he killed him."

"See, that was an accident. The van hit him too hard, flipped him clear across the street, and when he landed he cracked his skull open. It was a fucking mess," said Dickerson. "If Randy hadn't gotten the idea that...What's bothering that damn dog now?"

He glanced, frowning, at the draped windows. The chained hound was barking enthusiastically again.

"Did Randy leave town after Denby died?"

Dickerson frowned again at the draped window. "I hate dogs. If this was my place —"

"About Randy?"

"No, he decided it was safe to stay here. Denby was dead, and — damn that dog."

"Where's Randy now?"

"That ought to be worth extra."

"But it isn't," said Navarro. "Where is he?"

Sighing out smoke, he answered, "He's living with this girlfriend of his. Jesus, I don't know how he does it, but women are always taking him in."

"Where, exactly?"

"She's sort of rich, lives in a family mansion over in Orlando. Her folks are off in Europe, and they've got it to themselves," said the dealer. Slowly, looking down at the faded rug, he gave them the address.

The dog was barking even louder now.

Dickerson started to get up. "I better see what that fucker's so excited —"

The screen door creaked. Then the front door was kicked open.

13

"DON'T," ADVISED LES Janeiro as he crossed the threshold.

Navarro had been reaching inside his sport jacket toward the shoulder holster that held the .32 revolver he'd acquired since arriving in Florida. "Perhaps you're right." He clasped both hands in front of him.

The husky Janeiro was casually holding a .45 automatic in his right hand. Behind him loomed a tanned young man in designer jeans, gray sweatshirt and dark glasses. But he was not the same one they'd encountered at the Lakeside Dinner Theatre.

"Similar," observed Briggs.

Janeiro and the young man came farther into the small living room. "How's that?"

"You have similar — interchangeable — sidekicks."

"Trust the artist's eye to notice that."

"What the fuck are you guys doing busting into here?" asked Dickerson.

Ignoring him, Janeiro nodded at Navarro. "Mr. Klass would like to see you."

"As soon as we have a spare moment in our hectic schedule, we'll trot right over."

"Now, if you don't mind."

Navarro glanced over at his partner. "What say? Shall we comply with this request?"

"Obviously, Klass is anxious to get together with us. Let's."

"Okay, we may as well hit the road."

Janeiro gestured at Dickerson with his free hand. "We don't need you," he told him. "Just sit here for a while, don't phone anyone. Is that understood?"

Dickerson nodded.

"How'd you gents find us?" Navarro moved to the doorway.

"We have our ways."

"You didn't follow us from the hotel"

"No, that's true."

Dickerson said, "I sure as hell didn't invite them. I don't even know who these fuckers are."

"You go first, Mr. Navarro," said Janeiro, standing aside. "I'll escort you, and my associate will look after Mr. Briggs."

The dog was barking, snarling, lunging. He was out at the end of his chain, five feet from the gravel path that cut across the weedy yard. The orange tree quivered, and a woebegone orange dropped free and hit the ground with a mushy thunk.

Navarro was leading the single-file procession. When he was opposite the agitated hound, he apparently stumbled. He fell flat out and then went rolling back into Janeiro. That bowled the husky man over and sent him tumbling back, smack into the dog.

The animal got hold of his right arm and started worrying it. Popping to his feet, Navarro skittered across the high grass and grabbed the automatic that had shaken free of Janeiro's grasp.

Meantime, the second Navarro started to drop, Briggs had half-turned and crouched. Jabbing back with his elbow, he'd slammed the tan young man's crotch, hard, which had caused the latter to whoop and holler and forget about yanking out the .38 revolver tucked into the waistband of his tight jeans. Briggs hit him three times over the heart, extracting the gun at the same time.

"Stand quietly," he advised the gasping young man. "Rudy?"

Navarro had succeeded in shooing the dog off the fallen Janeiro. "Crawl back on to the path," he told him.

"This is one of my best suits. Now the sleeve's in tatters and that damn mutt slobbered all over me."

"I'll put you in touch with a very gifted invisible mender," promised Navarro.

"There was no need for all this rough-housing," Janeiro said, getting to his feet. "We are simply inviting you —"

"Listen, I want to see your boss," said Navarro. "Thing is, I get so embarrassed when I make an entrance with a goddamn automatic prodding my kidneys. Tell you what, *cabron*. You and your sidekick go on back to Klass. We'll tag along in our own vehicle."

"That's agreeable to me, and we could have arranged it without — "

"*Vamos*," suggested Navarro.

In the passenger seat, Briggs said, "That worked pretty well."

"Grandstanding is dumb," said Navarro, eyes on the maroon Cadillac they were following.

"Yet you did it."

"Doing dumb things now and then is one of the joys of life."

"I'm glad you tipped me off that you were going to make a move against those guys."

"I did?"

"Sure, you said 'hit the road.' That was an obvious allusion to the *Road* movies of Bob Hope and Bing Crosby," answered Briggs. "In those pictures they always pulled something on the heavies whenever they were in a jam."

"Bob Hope?" Navarro looked uncomprehending. "Is he the one with the moustache and cigar?"

"Okay, okay."

Navarro grinned.

Briggs said, "How'd Janeiro know we were at Dickerson's hideaway?"

"They didn't tail us," said Navarro. "And there is not a single electronic tracking dingus attached to this car."

"Dickerson didn't have any reason to contact Klass about us."

"I agree."

"Well, so?"

Navarro said, "Let me outline a possible scenario, *amigo*."

"Sure, go on."

"Klass — for reasons we'll soon learn — decides he wants to chew the fat with us and possibly shoot the breeze." Navarro swung the car over into the turn lane so they could keep on following Janeiro's car. "Klass dispatches these two goons over to our hotel to fetch us. We ain't there. But there's somebody there who does know where we went. And our goons know this person may know, and they — "

"Wait now. You're not going to suggest that Jenny Deacon knew where Dickerson was?"

"Didn't you tell her?"

"No, I sure as hell didn't, Rudy. Admittedly I was drunk last night, but...well, I'm pretty certain I didn't."

"Define 'pretty certain.'"

"During the part of the evening I can remember I'm sure I didn't."

"That leaves us the portion you can't dredge up out of the pool of memory."

"I suppose it's remotely possible I gave her his address. We did, sort of and in a way, talk about what I'm really up to here in Orlando. But only in very general terms."

"She was anxious to get you drunk. Think about why."

"Hey. 'Anxious' isn't the right word. Jenny didn't know about my problem with booze," said Briggs. "People meet on a vacation, and they hit it off. It's not sinister if one of them suggests having a friendly drink."

"Or a couple of dozen friendly drinks. Maybe not."

Briggs frowned. "C'mon, Rudy. Why would she want to know where Dickerson's hiding?"

"Possibly it has something to do with the fact that she's not Jenny Deacon."

There she was, sitting very still and straight, in a chair next to Klass's desk.

"I'm glad you could all make it," said Klass, who was clad in spotless tennis whites and perched on the edge of the desk.

"Jenny." Briggs hurried across the big office to her. "Why are you here?"

"I'm sorry, Jack, I had to tell them where you'd gone," she said quietly. "Did they hurt you?"

"No, actually we hurt them," he answered. "But how'd you know where we were?"

"You mentioned the address last evening."

Navarro settled, uninvited, into an armchair. "Planning to go over there later and dicker with Dickerson yourself, Jen?"

The auburn-haired young woman lowered her eyes, saying nothing.

Briggs crouched beside the chair. "Jenny, I'd appreciate it if you could explain just what in the hell is going on."

"Might I enter into the conversation?" Klass stood, nodded at his desk. The three Wisemann originals were laid out there, frames broken beside them and acetate torn. "The reason I wanted to talk to all three of you was—"

"Are you Jenny Deacon?" Briggs asked her.

"She's Jennifer Webb," said Klass. "I thought everybody knew that. She's been trying to get me to sell these drawings to her father's gallery. Now if we could continue?"

"Jennifer Webb?"

"At least the first name wasn't fake," said Navarro. "What happened to your drawings, Klass?"

Briggs eased up to his full height, then scowled down at the young woman. "I made a fool of myself over a woman again," he said. "You tracked me down at the damn hotel. You already knew who I was. You just pretended to like me. Hell, even that crap about my old paperback covers was faked. All an act so you could find out what the competition was up to."

"I really do like you, Jack," she insisted, reaching up and taking his hand. "I am Jenny Webb and I am after the Wisemann originals. But you have to believe me when I tell you that."

"How'd you know?" Briggs turned toward his partner.

"I called the Brimstone High School in rustic Brimstone, Connecticut. No Jenny Deacon on their staff—never has been."

"When did you call?"

"Day before yesterday."

"Oh, that's great. I'm the world's dumbest stalking horse. I'm the sheep they put out to lure the tiger, the cheese in the — "

"Quit mixing metaphors."

"I'm not mixing them. I'm merely stringing a bunch of them together, so as to illustrate what a schmuck I've been."

"Jack," said Jenny, "I was intending to — "

"Folks," interjected Klass, "what I'm even more interested in than this unfolding drama of romance and betrayal is who the devil broke into my office last night and messed with these Wisemann drawings."

Navarro said, "You have a fairly good security system, don't you?"

"Yes, but it was circumvented. By an expert."

"I could've done that," admitted Navarro. "But, hell, if we broke in here we'd have swiped the drawings. Our client wants all he can get."

Rubbing his palm with his fist, Klass said, "I am puzzled by that."

"The same goes for me," said Jenny. "Our gallery has several clients who want any and all Wisemanns we can come up with and no questions asked. Had I broken in — something I'm not capable of, since I don't have the electronic expertise Mr. Navarro apparently does — had I, however, I'd have swiped them all and express-mailed them to Boston. You have my word I didn't do this."

"And she's noted far and wide for her truthfulness," said Briggs. "Why's your desk lamp twisted around like that?"

Klass shrugged. "Burglar must've done it."

Briggs eased nearer the desk. The gooseneck lamp had been turned until its bulb pointed at the ceiling. He picked up one of the drawings and looked at it thoughtfully. "I got it," he said. "He must've been candling the drawings, holding them up to the light after breaking them out of their frames. But why do that?"

Navarro joined him, pointing a thumb at the lamp. "Explain a bit more."

"All of these originals were done on three- or four-ply drawing paper." Briggs turned on the lamp. "That means there are three or four separate layers of paper and something might've been concealed between the layers." He held the centaur drawing over the glaring bulb. "Nothing on this one."

Klass watched as he held the second and then third drawing to the light. "Something hidden? What do you mean?"

Clicking off the lamp, Briggs shook his head. "No sign of anything, and none of these has been split," he said. "You see, with a little skill and a lot of patience, Klass, you can separate the layers of this sort of paper. You could also soak a sheet in water and do it that way. Then you could slip something in between the plies and paste them back together again."

"Something like what, for instance?"

"Anything thin. A rare stamp, a drawing, a thousand dollar bill. I don't know."

"You think that's what the burglar was up to?" Klass asked.

"There's no way of telling for sure," answered Briggs. "But it seems likely that maybe something is hidden that way in the Wisemann drawings—or in only one of them—since your intruder took all three of them out of the frames and apparently held them to the light. Yet he didn't mess with the *Little Nemo* or anything else."

Klass nodded. "But what's it mean?"

"Means they've got two hundred and thirty-eight drawings to go," said Navarro.

"Huh?"

"Family joke, Klass. Can we depart?"

"Yes, go ahead," he said. "But let me tell you all something. From now on, if you want to see these drawings you'll have to go to my bank vault. That's where they'll be. A shame. They really brightened up my office."

Briggs said to Jenny, "You won't mind if we don't give you a lift back to the hotel?"

"I understand, Jack," she said. "I'm truly sorry this had to happen."

"I know, you're heartbroken." He walked out.

14

A SOFT, QUIET rain started right after they'd left their hotel.

Briggs concentrated on the wide, flat highway for a while. Eventually he inquired, "Want me to get some salsa music on the radio?"

"Here we see one of the root causes of ethnic prejudice at work," said Navarro.

"Huh?"

"Clean-cut yuppie type, feeling chagrined and guilt-ridden because of rolling in the hay with an attractive agent of the opposition, strikes out at upstanding, hardworking Chicano lad by suggesting his musical taste runs to stereotype."

"Okay," said Briggs. "I admit I was dumb."

"Could've happened to anyone."

"Nope, not to you. You would've checked up on Jenny — which, hell, you did anyway."

"I check up on everybody. Especially anyone who makes a point of getting to know my partner."

"She picked on me because I was the easier of the two to fool, right?"

"Our exit coming up."

"Oops." Swinging the wheel sharply, Briggs slid over into the right lane and flicked on the turn indicator. An angry horn sounded behind them. "Same to you, schmuck." Without looking back, he gave the honker the finger.

"You *gringos* are a fiery lot."

"It's stupid to do that, but gratifying." Briggs slowed as the car reached the off-ramp. "Story of my life. Most everything I do is stupid but gratifying. But, you know, Rudy, I figured Jenny liked me."

"Folks that sleep together don't actually have to like each other. I could cite you examples."

"Not the screwing part, but the other aspects. The conversations we had, her interest in art, even the way she smiled."

"Didn't most of your former wives impress you that way at one time, too?"

"Not really, no. I never thought most of them really liked me."

"Alas."

"Too much self-pity, you think?"

"No, no. It's just that when you talk about your tragic life my eyes cloud up with tears, and that makes it hard to read the damn street signs."

"I really am trying to reform," Briggs told him. "But drink and women are two of the world's biggest pitfalls."

"Turn left at the next corner."

Briggs did that. "Very impressive neighborhood," he noted, taking in the broad lawns and vast homes. Even on this gray afternoon everything seemed to glow and shine.

"That's the Duneen manse coming up on our right." Navarro nodded toward a white, vaguely Moorish house with a profusion of slanting red-tile roofs. It sat behind a high, stucco wall at the crest of a half-acre of green lawn.

"Shirley Ann Duneen," said Briggs. "I read about her in the columns up in Manhattan a few times. She's what the late show movies would call a madcap heiress."

"With faulty taste in beaus."

"We haven't yet seen Randy Sunn. He may well be a charming fellow."

"He's more than likely the scruffy blond guy that comic-shop lady told you was trying to sell her further Wisemann originals."

"Scruffy people sometimes have charisma."

"Park around the next corner."

Briggs parked beneath a palm tree. The rain hit lightly at them as they got out of the car.

Navarro said, "We can cut across the back acreage of this place, skirt yonder little lake and come up on the Duneen house from the back."

He started walking, stepped over a low hedge and onto a neatly cropped lawn. A half-dozen sprinklers were at work, snicking and spraying.

"It must be nice to be wealthy," observed Briggs. "That way you don't have to depend on anything as common as rain for watering your lawn."

They didn't encounter anyone while making their way along the shore of the lake. Tied to a small blue-painted dock was a weathered rowboat with *Golden Vanity* lettered on its prow.

The back lawn of the Duneen estate hadn't been mowed for at least a month, and the grass was ankle high. Navarro halted a few steps into it and scanned the rear sprawl of the house. Then he went trudging toward the four-car garage on his left.

Briggs got to the garage first and looked in one of its small dusty side windows. "The van is in here," he said quietly. "There's a lemon on the side panel sporting dark glasses. This is the Blind Lemon van, Rudy. Rudy?"

"Over here, *amigo*." Navarro was crouched by a red-flowered bush.

"What's the — Oh, shit!"

Sprawled on the other side of the bushes was a German shepherd. Its throat had been recently cut.

Navarro eased his .32 revolver from its shoulder holster. "We're still going into this place," he said. "But we'll be *muy* careful."

They moved through the rain to the back door. While they were still thirty feet away, a young woman cried out in pain from someplace inside the mansion. Jack started to run toward the house. Navarro caught up with him and grabbed his arm.

"Caution is what's needed, *amigo*."

The girl screamed again. It was a long, thin cry.

"That's not a fake, Rudy."

"Even so." Navarro approached the door, eyes narrowing. "Somebody broke in this way."

"He took a position to the left of the door, reached out and yanked it open.

Nothing happened.

Navarro ventured a look. "Okay, thus far." He entered.

Briggs followed. They were in a large white kitchen. The room smelled of spaghetti, stale pizza, aging vegetables and cigarettes. Plates crusted with deep-red sauce, gravy and something unidentifiable but orangish were scattered atop a round, raw-wood table. The sink was rich with unwashed dishes, and several fat black flies circled low above the mound. Half of a tomato sat on the white tile floor in front of the pale yellow refrigerator, and three crumpled cloth napkins rested near it.

"They must have the same decorator you do," said Navarro quietly.

There was another scream. A woman's voice pleaded, "Please, no. Please."

Briggs pointed at the ceiling. "Upstairs."

Nodding, Navarro slipped out into a long, white hallway.

A pair of black pantyhose dangled from one of the dark metal wall lamps half-way along the corridor, and a guitar case leaned against the off-white wall a little farther along.

Navarro, gun in hand, moved quietly. At the end of the hall was the heavy, oaken front door. A stairway with a wrought-iron railing led up to the next floor.

Briggs was watching his partner and didn't notice all that was underfoot. He didn't see a blue canvas deck shoe until he'd tripped over it. He stumbled, bumped into the wall with a loud thunk and knocked over the guitar case. It toppled and hit the floor with a twangy thud.

Less than a minute later a dark figure in a windbreaker and ski mask appeared on the stairs. Not saying a word, he fired down with a .45 automatic.

15

"HIT THE DECK," advised Navarro, ducking, dropping to a crouch and firing up at the rapidly descending figure.

The first shot from the automatic had whizzed through the spot where he'd been and slammed into the hallway wall.

"I already thought of that on my own." Briggs was flat out on the carpeting.

The man in the ski mask came thudding the rest of the way down the stairs. He fired two more shots in Navarro's direction, then ran straight for the front door, yanked it open and dived out into the rain.

Navarro rose up from the sprawl he'd gone into because of the last shots. Out through the open door he could see the big man jogging across the wet grass. Water splashed up as he ran, and he went clean over the stucco wall as though it were a minor hurdle in an obstacle course.

"We'll let him go," said Navarro. "You okay, Jack?"

"I'd like some time to frame a reply." Taking a deep breath, he got to his feet. "Christ, I'm not used to this kind of work."

"Neither am I, *amigo*."

"Haven't you ever been shot at?"

"Sure, several times," he answered. "But it's not something you get used to." Easing over to the foot of the stairs, Navarro looked up.

From somewhere on the second floor came the sound of a low, hopeless whimpering.

The young woman was alive. The lean, blond young man on the blood-spattered bed wasn't.

The pink drapes of the big bedroom were shut tight, and everything had a blurred, shadowy look. The room was too hot, and it smelled of spilled perfume and burned flesh.

"Jesus," said Briggs, hesitating in the doorway.

The young woman was blonde and tan, naked, and tied to a straight-back kitchen chair with green plastic clothesline. She was leaning far to the left, and only the cords wrapped tight around her body kept her from falling from the chair. There were raw, ugly splotches on her arms, on her breasts and all down her right thigh.

"I really don't know where it is," she murmured, eyes nearly closed.

Her face was zigzagged with streaks of blood, and the skin around her left eye was red and swollen. Blood had splashed her hair and was turning to black clots.

Navarro, after scanning the room, put his gun away. "Miss Duneen?" he said softly, crossing to her.

"Please. Please, don't hurt me anymore."

"It's okay, it's okay." He fished a pocket knife out of his pocket. "We're on your side. I'll just cut — "

"Please!" She screamed as she stared down at the open knife. "Please believe me! I don't know where the trunk is."

"I'm just going to get you loose from these ropes." He dropped the hand holding the knife to his side, crouched beside her. "Okay?"

There was blood all around her mouth. "He was going to put the knife inside — "

"It's all right now, trust me." Very gently, he began to slice at the line holding her ankles together.

"I don't know where the trunk is."

"Did Randy know?"

"Yes. He wanted Randy to tell, but Randy wouldn't."

"You know who this guy was?" He had her legs freed.

"No. No, we were in bed, Randy and I. We were in bed, making, you know, love…and this man just walked right in. He had a gun, and he was carrying a chair from down in the kitchen.

That seemed so...strange. Funny and frightening at the same time. A man in a ski mask bursting into your bedroom carrying a chair. He had a gun and he made Randy tie me to the chair. He brought a roll of clothesline, too. Did I tell you that? Like you buy at the supermarket. That was funny, too. He tied Randy up himself, arms and legs pulled up behind him, and dumped him on the bed and...Oh, Jesus, God. Randy wouldn't tell him, wouldn't tell him where the trunk was."

"Easy now." Navarro was cutting away the ropes around her torso. He had to be careful because of the cigarette burns and knife slashes.

Very carefully, Briggs finally came into the bedroom. Not looking at the man on the bed, he went over to the closet.

The girl said, "He hit Randy, and burned him, and God, I don't know...Randy could be so damn stubborn. He knew those drawings were valuable and didn't want this man to have them. The man did...something to Randy's...to his balls with the knife...Oh, Jesus, Randy yelled so bad, and then he just died. His heart...He had a heart thing, but he didn't believe it was that serious. I told him he could see one of Mother's doctors and it wouldn't...you know, it wouldn't even cost anything. But he was...he didn't want to see anybody. Doesn't matter now. He died. Then the man started on me."

Navarro lifted away the last of the ropes. "Is the trunk in the house?"

"No. Randy was upset about it, about all the trouble it was causing him. He shipped it off someplace. I told the man that, but he wouldn't believe me." She swayed and started to fall from the chair.

Navarro caught her by the arm.

She grimaced with pain and passed out.

Shirley Ann Duneen, wearing the pale blue robe Briggs had found for her in the closet of the master bedroom, sat in an armchair in the small bedroom that had been hers as a child.

"Thanks for...Forgive me, I don't feel so well." She bent, grimacing. "I wanted to thank you...If he hadn't heard you, if you hadn't gotten here..."

"My partner's calling the police and an ambulance." Briggs was sitting on the edge of the bed next to a large panda doll.

"I still don't understand how you got here. Are you police, too?"

"Not exactly." Briggs tried a reassuring smile. "We're private detectives. Or at least Navarro is. I'm a special consultant."

She hugged herself but found that was painful, too. "You were looking for Randy?"

"And the Wisemann drawings."

"His wife's family hired you?"

"Nope, someone else."

"I really don't know where that trunk is now."

"But it was here?"

"Until a few days ago. Then Randy got worried because... Well, he got worried and took it away. He told me he shipped it to a friend."

Briggs said, "We know about Denby."

"Who?"

"Guy Randy hit with his van."

"He didn't mean to kill him."

"Probably not."

"I guess it doesn't make one hell of a lot of difference now, anyway. Randy's dead, too."

Briggs tapped his fingers absently on the panda's stomach. It produced a bleating noise. "Oops, sorry."

"I really don't have much sense when it comes to men."

"It can be the same way when it comes to women," Briggs said. "I've had three wives."

"So has my stepfather. But he's older than you." She glanced at the open doorway. "How long do you think it'll take the ambulance to get here?"

"Not too long. Navarro has connections."

"He's from around here?"

"No, but he knows people."

94

She leaned far forward, biting at her lower lip. "Those aspirins you gave me sure aren't helping much."

"Didn't expect they would. But sometimes they have a placebo effect."

"Not this time. Jesus, it hurts."

"They'll be here soon."

"Will they arrest me?"

"Nope."

"But I'm an accessory or something. I knew Randy had killed that man."

"Tell 'em you didn't know."

Shirley Ann said, "But *you* know."

"We have no reason to mention that to anyone," Briggs told her. "And you're forgetting that you're an important person hereabouts. Fine family, money, so on. They'll be nice to you. Especially when your lawyers talk to them."

"That's an idea." She sat up. "I better call Oscar. That's Oscar Winwood, Mother's lawyer, and mine, too, sometimes."

"Give me his number and I'll phone him for you." He stood.

"You're very helpful."

"Yes, it's one of my better traits."

Outside, sirens could be heard.

16

"LISTEN, YOU DIMINUTIVE son of a bitch, I want less crap and more — "

"*Madre de dios*," complained Navarro from a kitchen chair, "you're causing me to lose face in front of my old school chum. Here I tell him that ours was once one of the great romances of the Western world, and then you treat me like this."

"Briggs?" The blonde police detective snorted. "He's a twerp, same as you."

"Guilt by association." Briggs was leaning against the Duneen refrigerator. "Mother warned me that if I hung around with twerps long enough I'd be labeled one myself."

"He's as big an asshole as you," she told Navarro. "Now I want to know what this is all about." She pointed a thumb at the ceiling. "We've got a homicide, an attempted homicide, a possible rape, and you two halfwits in the middle of it."

Navarro coughed into his hand. "Allow me, Kate, to straighten you out," he offered. "Technically, the dead man upstairs may have died of a heart attack. Nobody was trying to kill Shirley Ann Duneen or rape her."

"I supposed this masked intruder didn't torture them either?"

"That he did do. What he was after was information."

"About what?"

Navarro nodded at his friend.

Briggs answered, "The Wisemann originals."

Kate frowned at him. "He tortured these people, killed one of them, all for a few drawings?"

"Could be more than a few," said Briggs.

"How many?"

"We don't know," said Navarro.

"What does the dead man have to do with the Wisemann stuff?"

"He allegedly stole some of the drawings," said Navarro. "He's been trying to sell them. I've already filled you in on all that business about the three drawings showing up."

"And you told me each one was worth maybe $10,000 tops. Some guy in a ski mask is going to commit murder for a hundred thousand worth of cartoons?"

"C'mon, Kate. You've got junkies who'll kill somebody for ten bucks."

"Okay, but I still —"

"Pardon me, Detective McBride." A black uniformed officer was in the kitchen doorway. "We found something out in the garage."

"What, Rosco?"

"A van that looks like it may be the one involved in that hit-and-run."

"Navarro, did you know about that goddamn van?"

He studied the ceiling. "I was coming to that."

She glared. "Now would be a dandy time to tell me."

"It seems likely that Randy Sunn is responsible for the hit-and-run death of Norm Denby."

"Was it an accident, or did he have a reason for killing him?"

Navarro spread his hands wide. "I have no idea, hon."

Resting both elbows on the coffee shop table, Navarro said, "Okay, we're now a safe distance from the scene of the crime."

"None of this quite makes sense." Briggs was stirring sugar into his coffee. "Not to me."

"It makes some."

"Randy Sunn is married to a relative of Coulthard's, right?"

"Such is the case, yes. I checked on it."

"Okay, and he swiped the trunk and brought it here to Florida with him in his Blind Lemon van."

"Also true. The drawings Klass bought came from the trunk.

There were a lot more of them in there, according to Shirley Ann Duneen."

"So what exactly are we experiencing here, a little science fiction interlude? Have we wandered into an alternate universe where the trunk didn't vanish back in the forties and Coulthard kept it?"

Navarro took a sip of his herb tea. "*Chihuahua! Muy malo*," he commented. "Back to your query. What we're in is the same old universe, Jack, wherein folks scheme and lie."

"Coulthard lied about the trunk disappearing? Why? Did he collect insurance?"

"He did, yes. But he maybe had other motives."

"Such as?"

Navarro looked out the steamy window at the rain. Along the narrow side street a glazier's truck was rattling. The big slanted panes of glass it was carrying sparkled with raindrops. "I'm working up a list of possible reasons."

"Another thing I don't quite understand is why'd the guy who broke into Klass's office just hold the Wisemann originals up to the light and not swipe them?"

"You already answered that one."

"I suggested there might be a message hidden between the layers of the paper. You think that's possible?"

"There's something." With an impatient shake of his head, Navarro reached into the breast pocket of his sport coat. "Now let's look at what I withheld from Detective K.T. McBride."

"She is tall, isn't she?"

"Taller than I." Navarro produced a folded slip of yellow paper and a folded letter. He unfurled the slip and smoothed it out on the table next to his mug of vile tea.

"She's obviously fond of you, though. If you don't listen to her words and just look in her eyes, you'll tell she actually — "

"Feast your eyes on this, will you?"

"Hey, a shipping company receipt." Briggs picked it up. "The trunk was sent to this address in New Paltz, New York. Six days ago."

"The damn thing moves around more than the Maltese Falcon or the Holy Grail." Navarro retrieved the receipt. "I found this in Randy's wallet. The wallet was in his pants, and they were tossed behind a chair in the bedroom." Folding the slip, he returned it to his pocket. "We'll check out of our posh hotel and wend our way to New Paltz. A real garden spot, from all I hear."

"Are we allowed to leave Florida?"

"Sure, K.T. won't detain us in any way."

Briggs tapped the letter. "And what's this?"

"That was also in the wallet, wadded up with a condom, a Japanese coin and some flecks of inferior pot. Read it."

Briggs scanned the letter. "This must be what first gave Randy Sunn the notion the Wisemann originals were valuable."

"No doubt, since he wasn't an expert on graphic arts."

Briggs set the letter down. "A little over a year ago, this Dr. Kathleen Starlin — I imagine she's a Ph.D. and not a medic — a year or so ago, she writes to Randy's wife as heir of the late Coulthard. The doctor's been doing research — apparently the first to do so — in the papers of Mrs. Heinrich Wisemann, which were donated to the Boston Graphics College back in 1967, when the widow expired."

"Yep, and Dr. Starlin wondered if Mrs. Sunn had any papers, notes or drawings of Heinrich Wisemann."

"You think they ever responded to her?"

"Probably not. Since they weren't supposed to have the damn trunk at all."

"Our list of people interested in the drawings keeps growing."

"We can add Dr. Starlin and the gent in the ski mask."

"Could he be this MacQuarrie guy who's in Orlando looking for the drawings, too?"

"Not unless MacQuarrie padded that outfit considerably. I talked to him yesterday. He's about my size," said Navarro. "Now let me ask you something. Did you tell anyone we were going to call on Randy Sunn and where he was living?"

"Of course not." Briggs frowned, angry. "Jesus, Rudy, you were with me most of the time since we found out where he was.

You think that I slipped the address to Jenny or something?"

"Just checking."

"Seems an asshole trick to me, checking on your own partner."
Briggs got up. "I'll see you in the car." He went striding out of
the restaurant.

17

BRIGGS WAS TOSSING his wallet and room key on the desk when he noticed the phone in the mirror. The tiny red light on its base was flashing. Sitting on the edge of the bed, he punched "0."

"Hotel Orlando Rococco."

"Jack Briggs. Is there a message for me?"

"Just a moment, Mr. Briggs."

He glanced toward his window. The day was ending, and darkness was closing in.

"Mr. Briggs. A Miss Jenny Webb called you twice. She left a message. Shall I read it?"

"Yeah, go ahead."

" 'Have moved to Fantasy Castle Motel on International Drive. Have important information for you. Please call. 555-1587, room sixteen.' Shall I repeat that?"

"Nope, I've assimilated it. Thanks." He hung up, went through the ritual of getting an outside line and punched out Jenny's number.

"Fantasy Castle."

"Jenny Webb, room sixteen, please."

"That line is busy, sir."

"Okay, thanks." Briggs hung up and walked over to the window. He did a few knee bends. He straightened, then discovered he could still touch his toes. "Maybe I can win back the title of World's Most Perfectly Developed Man."

He tried Jenny three more times in the next fifteen minutes. The number continued to be busy.

He made another try five minutes later with the same result.

He left his room then, journeyed along the hall to Navarro's, and knocked.

"*Quién es?*"

"Me."

The door opened. "I thought you'd still be sulking in your tent." Navarro wandered back inside.

"Something's come up."

"Jenny, huh?"

"How'd you know?"

"Many years ago in Tibet I learned the trick of reading faces." Navarro sat again at the round table by his window and picked up a hotel pen. "The hangdog expression you're wearing indicates perplexity over a lady."

"She's checked out of this hotel."

"Afraid to face us, obviously. For other parts?"

"No, she checked into a motel a few minutes from here. Place called the Fantasy Castle."

"Sounds like a four-star operation. And?"

"When I got back, there was a message. She said she has important information."

"You want me to tie you to the mast to keep you from returning the call?"

"I've been trying to phone her for about a half hour. Line keeps being busy."

"With romance as with sleuthing, *amigo,* patience is a virtue."

"I'm sort of worried. What with this guy in the ski mask running loose."

"Why would he want to interfere with the course of true love?"

"I'm sure Jenny wants to talk to me about something that has to do with the Wisemann originals."

Navarro picked up a set of keys from the table. "Go over to the Fantasy Castle and see her." He tossed the keys.

Briggs caught them. "She really may have something valuable to pass along."

"Okay, but don't take all night finding out what it is," said

Navarro. "I got us booked on a flight for New York at nine *mañana*."

It almost looked like a castle there in the night. A stunted, woebegone castle, but a castle. There was a turret with a tattered pennant, a miniature drawbridge and a weedy courtyard. A suit of armor, more than likely made of plastic, stood on guard next to the entrance of the visitors' parking lot.

Briggs parked and started hunting for Room 16. The room was at the back of the shadowy courtyard, on the ground floor. The drapes were drawn but light showed through.

"...renewed fighting broke out all along the border today as the two factions in this prolonged conflict moved to..." The television set was talking inside the motel room.

Briggs knocked.

"...White House denied any knowledge of that assassination and a spokesman stated there is no CIA involvement in this key Latin American—"

"Jenny?" He knocked harder.

The force of his knocking caused the unlocked door to swing open about a foot.

"Jenny? It's Jack."

He hesitated about ten seconds before nudging the door all the way open, then he waited another ten before going in. He recognized Jenny at once, even looking as she did.

She was wearing a pair of white jeans and nothing else. Her ankles were bound with green plastic clothesline, her arms tied behind her back. She was lying on her side. A black plastic garbage bag had been pulled over her head and taped tightly in place.

Briggs didn't see any sign that she was still breathing.

18

"THANKS, I APPRECIATE the help." Navarro hung up the phone.

He stretched out on his bed. "Hotel pillows are never fat enough." He reached over to the other side of the bed, grabbed the spare pillow, and added it to the one he was trying to recline against.

Locking his hands behind his head, he contemplated the ceiling thoughtfully.

The phone rang.

"*Sí?*"

"Rudy," said Briggs, "you'd best come over here."

"To the Fantasy Castle?"

"Yep." Briggs gave the address.

"You sound a shade uneasy, *amigo.*"

"Can't discuss that over the phone."

"You okay?"

"I am, yes."

"What about Jenny?"

"More or less."

"Much as I enjoy suspense, I'll ring off now," said Navarro, sitting up. "I'll catch a cab."

"That's a splendid idea, Rudy."

"*Adiós.*" Navarro put on his shoes, which had been sitting neatly side by side next to the bed. "I'd been thinking about dropping over there anyway."

Navarro said, "We better get you to a doctor."

"No," said Jenny.

"Being deprived of oxygen for even—"

"It was only a matter of seconds. Jack got here just as he went out the back window." She was sitting in a maroon armchair, wearing a long terry robe. Her face was very pale, her eyes underlined with shadow. "I don't need a doctor—nor any police."

"I wasn't suggesting cops."

"Going to a doctor and telling him somebody tried to asphyxiate me would sure as hell prompt him to notify the police."

"Not the doctor I know."

"I've been with her a half hour or more, Rudy." Briggs was leaning against the wall near the young woman's chair. "She seems to be all right."

Navarro puckered his cheek. "Who was it?"

"The guy in the ski mask," answered Briggs.

"You saw him?"

"No, but Jenny described him. It has to be the same guy who killed Randy Sunn."

Navarro sat on the edge of the disordered bed. "You told her about that?"

"You'd better listen to what she has to say, Rudy. It all ties in, and she's pretty certain she knows who he is."

"Who?"

Jenny shook her head. "Let me tell this my way," she requested, picking up a Styrofoam cup of coffee. "Or, Jack, maybe you can explain some of it to him. I'm starting to get a terrific headache."

"Maybe you ought to lie down."

"Not on that bed."

"He tied her up and left her on the bed," said Briggs.

"Lucky he didn't lock the door while he was going about his work."

"He didn't have time," Jenny said. "He forced his way in here and hit me. I was just about unconscious before I could even scream. Then he tied me up. I came to just as Jack was taking that awful bag off me."

"Lucky again," said Navarro.

"Maybe you'd like it better if he'd succeeded in suffocating her.

Then there'd be less competition for the Wisemann originals."

"Jack, just tell me the story."

Briggs was frowning. "Rudy, we know this guy is a killer. So why are you—"

"Excuse it," said Navarro, grinning. "I sometimes overreact under stress. I apologize. Proceed."

Jenny said, "I will admit I haven't been completely honest with you till now."

"*Es posible?*"

"I mean, even after I admitted that I was really Jennifer Webb and sent down here by my father," she went on. "What I'm getting at is that I haven't told you everything."

Briggs said, "It has to do with Dr. Kathleen Starlin."

"The lady from Boston Graphics U. The one who wrote the letter to Randy's missus."

"That Dr. Kathleen Starlin, yes," said Briggs. "When I mentioned her name to Jenny, she decided she better tell me what she knows about the woman. She is a Ph.D., by the way. A woman in her forties, on the dumpy side. She's been doing research on the life of Heinrich Wisemann for the past three years or so."

"Naturally, since my father and I know quite a bit about Wisemann's work, she started dropping in at the shop," said Jenny. "She and I became friends. She confided in me, and I'm afraid I confided in her."

"Those papers of Marthe Wisemann's turn out to have some interesting stuff in them," picked up Briggs. "It's incredible, but apparently all true. Changes my whole perception of Wisemann."

Navarro said, "So tell me about it."

"I'm feeling a little better," said Jenny, sipping at her coffee. "I didn't tell Jack all the details before you got here. Perhaps I'd better explain this after all, Jack."

"Sure, if you're up to it."

"Yes, I am," she said. "Wisemann's widow, according to what Kathleen Starlin told me, was a very bitter woman in her final years. She died in 1967. The college in Boston had her papers and journals for a long time, crated up in a basement, before anyone bothered to take a look. Kathleen was the first person to systematically go through everything. What she found out was — "

"Wisemann was a Nazi," said Briggs.

"Eh?" Navarro bounced once on the bed.

"If what his widow asserts is true, and I have no reason to doubt it," said the young woman. "From the middle 1930s onward Wisemann was a high-ranking Nazi in good standing."

"A Jewish Nazi?"

"He apparently wasn't a Jew. That was a story planted later on," she said. "Because of his artistic background, Wisemann was one of those — and a fairly important one of those — who helped amass a substantial collection of art treasures from occupied countries during the war. Paintings, sculpture, engravings, rare books. Marthe Wisemann estimated the value of the wartime loot Wisemann was involved with at about twenty million dollars. Now, obviously, those art treasures are worth many times that."

"If the Allies didn't long since find them."

"They didn't," she assured Navarro. "Mrs. Wisemann put enough details in her journals to make it obvious that much of that material was never found after the end of the Second World War. Wisemann, for instance, was especially fond of French Impressionist paintings. The canvases his widow mentions are still believed lost."

"Okay," said Navarro, "so where'd he stash them?"

"The unit of looters Wisemann was in charge of buried most of the treasures in rural Germany. She's not specific as to exactly where."

Navarro brightened. "Ah," he said, "I get it now. Wisemann drew a map, showing where the stuff was hidden."

Nodding, Jenny said, "A very detailed map. He did, as Jack suspected, hide it between the layers of paper in one of his old drawings. Again, Marthe Wisemann doesn't say which drawing he split and reassembled. But apparently, between the layers of one of the drawings in that trunk, there's a pencilled map. Shortly before the fall of Hitler, Wisemann was smuggled out of Germany. The concentration camp story was already in circulation to cover him. He got to America about the time the war in Europe ended and set up a new identity."

"The tell-tale drawing, along with the couple hundred others, was left behind in the trunk. Once Wisemann was well established here, the trunk was to be sent to him," said Briggs. "And eventually he'd send for his wife. When everything looked safe, they'd go back home to Germany and dig up the loot."

"Since the story about Wisemann dying in a concentration camp had been well planted, the Allies never bothered Mrs. Wisemann," added Jenny. "At the end of the war they treated her very well."

"Coulthard had to be in on it," said Navarro.

"From what Mrs. Wisemann wrote, it's certain he was," said Jenny. "But only to the extent that he knew about Wisemann's Nazi connections and that he was still alive and hiding out in the United States."

"But not about the buried loot?"

She shook her head. "They never told him about that at all," she answered. "Coulthard thought he was just helping out an artist whom he admired. He'd see the trunk got safely out of Germany and found its way to Wisemann."

"Jenny thinks," came in Briggs, "that the trunk was delivered to Wisemann and that Coulthard's story about its being lost was a cover-up."

"So how'd the damn trunk end up in the Coulthard family attic?"

Jenny said, "Wisemann must've died sometime in the fifties. Before he was able to get back to Germany or send for his wife."

"Never hearing from him after a certain point," added Briggs, "she assumed he'd abandoned her. Hence the nasty jottings in her journals."

Navarro got up and commenced pacing. "Suppose the old broad was just dotty in her final days and made this all up?"

"The details sound right. They're convincing," said Jenny. "At least Kathleen Starlin thinks so. I'm not anywhere near the expert she is."

"What about Coulthard?" asked Navarro.

"We know he died in 1956," answered Jenny. "If, as Dr. Starlin surmises, Wisemann died prior to that, then it seems likely Coulthard retrieved the trunk somehow. Or he may have been holding it all the time, waiting for Wisemann to contact him."

"He may also have found the map."

"I don't think so, from what Kathleen told me." She held her cup in both hands. "His family didn't seem to know. They didn't even realize the Wisemann originals themselves were of any particular value."

"Nazi treasure," said Navarro as he paced. "I never have worked on a case involving genuine Nazi treasure before. I'll be the envy of all the other kids on the block."

"It makes sense, Rudy," said Briggs. "If we're talking about a hundred million dollars' worth of wartime loot, that gives the guy in the ski mask a hell of a good motive."

"And who is he?" Navarro halted near Jenny.

"I think, although I can't exactly prove it, that he's a man named Wes Marzlov," she said. "I didn't find out until too late that Kathleen Starlin was somewhat disturbed, mentally. Marzlov is her lover, and a man with a long history of violence."

Briggs asked, "They're teamed up on this?"

"Yes, and I'm afraid it's my fault. I was so excited when we found out there might be a cache of drawings here in Orlando that I told Kathleen about it." Jenny set her cup aside, frowning. "Naive of me, but I guess I still wanted to believe she was just a dedicated Wisemann scholar. Obviously — at least it's obvious now — she's much more interested in finding that map."

"A hundred million has been known to corrupt the most dedicated of scholars," said Navarro. "Is Dr. Starlin in the vicinity?"

"I doubt it, since she has a fear of flying. My guess is that Kathleen sent Marzlov down here. The man who attacked me, I'm almost certain it was him."

"Assuming he is our masked marvel," said Navarro, "why would Marzlov want you dead?"

She looked up at him, her face still very pale. "That should be obvious. To keep me from telling you exactly what I'm telling you now."

"Jenny's also in competition with them in the hunt for the originals," Briggs pointed out.

"So are we."

"Marzlov will probably try to kill you, too," she said quietly.

"Listen, Rudy," said Briggs, "I haven't told Jenny where we're heading next. But I think it might be safer for her if she came along with us. We can probably work out something when we find the trunk. So many originals for our client, so many for Jenny and her father. I know that's maybe against Ajax Novelty policy, but — "

"You two know where the trunk is?" Jenny sat up in her chair.

Navarro smiled. "That we do, Jennifer," he said amiably. "And I must say I think Jack's come up with a splendid notion here. Yes, we'll all be safer if we team up."

She watched him for a few silent seconds. "You really mean that?"

"You have the word of a Navarro." He shuffled over to the door. "Jack, you'd better stay and look after her tonight." He held out his hand. "I'll take the car and meet you back here at six sharp *mañana*."

Briggs dug the car keys out of his trouser pocket. "If you don't mind my staying, Jenny?"

"No, I'd like that."

Smiling, Navarro opened the door. "I'll see about reserving you a seat on our flight, Jennifer," he said. "Keep in mind, Jack, that we'll have to get back to the Rococco in time to get your stuff packed in the morning."

"I can pack in a few minutes."

"*Vaya con dios*, kiddies," he said and departed.

19

BRIGGS KNOCKED AGAIN on the motel-room door. "Jenny?" There was no response.

He hit the door several times with his fist, then tried the knob. The door was locked.

"Jenny, are you okay?"

"Yes." The chain rattled, the door opened. "I was in the bathroom, finishing dressing. Sorry."

She was wearing jeans and a cablestitch sweater. Her auburn hair was pulled back and held with a twist of green ribbon.

Briggs entered, holding the pizza box in front of him. "I got to thinking, while I was waiting on the doorstep, that my going out to pick up food for us wasn't an especially bright idea."

"I kept the door locked and chained." She took the box and the paper bag he was carrying. "Orange juice?"

"We're in Florida, after all. And I'm off booze."

"That's right. I forgot." She placed everything on the low coffee table. "Seems very unlikely that Marzlov would come back tonight. After you practically caught him in the act."

"I suppose." He tugged the quart carton of juice out of the sack.

"While I was dressing, I remembered something — something about Marzlov." She returned to the bathroom and came back with two glasses. "Very best plastic."

"I'll pour," he said. "What about Marzlov?"

"Kathleen mentioned once that he comes from a fairly prominent Boston family." She set the glasses on the table. "They're in the electronics business, and while Marzlov is sort of the black sheep of the family, he knows a lot about electronic gadgets."

"The kind used to bug rooms, tap phones and otherwise listen in?"

She nodded, picking up the glass of juice he'd poured for her. "Yes, and that could mean he's been spying on us all along, not only with bugs but with sonic guns and sophisticated things like that."

"That might explain how the guy's anticipated us now and then."

She sat in one of the two flowered chairs. "I think it's all right to talk now. There aren't any gadgets in this room. I made sure of that," she said. "It's unlikely he'd be lurking around outside either. So he can't know we're going to New Paltz, or about that music shop where Randy Sunn supposedly shipped the trunk."

"Not unless he was crouched down in the shrubs with a sonic device when I told you about that." He took the other chair. "Are you especially hungry?"

"Not at the moment."

"Neither am I. Although it sounded like a nifty idea when you first suggested my going out for something."

Standing, she came over and took his hand. "What I'd like to do, Jack, is just have you hold me for a while."

He got up, put his arms around her. "I can do that. It's one of the things I learned in school."

"I'm very afraid," she admitted, resting her head against his chest. "I could've died tonight. I came so damn close to it."

Briggs bent and kissed her.

It started raining on Navarro. He stepped out of the parked car just as the first drops fell from the blurred night sky.

"*Caramba*," he said aloud, starting doubletime across the hotel parking lot.

He was carrying a small paper bag that held the container of plain yogurt and the apple that he'd purchased at an all-night mom and pop on the way home. Beyond a cyclone fence stretched the broad hotel lawn. In its center was the swimming pool, lit up by its underwater lights. It looked like a giant sheet of marbled paper fluttering in the air.

"You're getting too poetic, *muchacho*," he warned himself as he started down the graveled path cutting across the lawn to the hotel. "Keep in mind, *por favor,* that metaphors and similes lead you away from reality and not closer to...*Chihuahua!*"

Navarro flung away his yogurt sack and dove groundward.

Beside the pool some hundred feet away a dark figure was rising. A husky man in dark clothes and a ski mask. He held a .45 automatic.

His first shot missed the low, scurrying Navarro by several yards. Navarro rolled across the wet grass, tugging out his revolver.

The next slug from the masked man's gun hit just four or five feet to Navarro's right.

"*Cabron!*" He suddenly jumped to his feet. Standing wide-legged and gripping his gun in both hands, he fired swiftly and carefully.

Nothing at all seemed to happen for about five seconds. Then the man in the ski mask hopped backward, made some personal semaphore signals with both arms, and lurched to his right.

"Holy shit," observed Navarro, knowing what was coming up.

The gunman fell back into the lighted pool.

Navarro sprinted over to the edge and spotted a long pole with a hook on the end of it. Holstering his gun, he grabbed up the pole and squatted at the edge.

But there was nothing to do. The gunman was doing a dead man's float out near the deep end. It wasn't an act. He was truly and completely dead.

"Damn, I wanted to talk to this guy."

Navarro shook his head, dropped the pole and started walking backward. He sat in a damp deck chair, watching the rain hit at the floating body.

Police noise filled the area around the pool. Uniformed cops, plainclothes cops and medics mingled.

"You little asshole," Detective Kate McBride was saying to Navarro. "That bastard could've killed you."

"Such was his avowed intent, I do believe." Navarro was sitting in a deck chair — a different one than earlier — at the edge of the activity.

Kate was sitting in a canvas chair next to him. "His name is Ernie Quesada."

"Another Latino, huh?"

"From Cuba. A hired gun sort of fellow."

Navarro nodded. "Never heard of him."

"He's a local at the moment," she said. "Now suppose you explain why somebody hired Quesada to kill you."

"Well, Katie, I have to admit that sometimes I'm a bit free with my tongue. It does rile an occasional — "

"C'mon, no bullshit."

"I have no notion."

"You think he was just sitting here, planning to shoot at the first twerp who came strolling along?"

"Makes sense to me. There's an awful lot of anti-twerp sentiment in your part of Florida."

"Rudy, lying right over yonder is a big husky guy in dark clothing. He's wearing a ski mask."

"True. That's true."

"Quesada fits the description of the man you say killed Randy Sunn and tortured the Duneen girl."

"Most ski masks look alike to me."

"Are you saying he's not the same guy you ran into at the Duneen place?"

"No, *chiquita*. I am merely saying I don't know."

She sighed a very thorough sigh. "Quesada never struck me as a collector of cartoons."

"Kate, I'll explain this once again," said Navarro. "I parked the jalopy, started down along the path toward the hotel here. All I had in mind was watching an X-rated movie while consuming my plain yogurt. I note this goon occupying that candy-striped chair over there. He pops up, aims his gun at me and shoots. I drop down, turn around and shoot back. The result is — "

118

"Why? Why's somebody want you dead?"

"*Quién sabe?*"

"Stop playing wetback with me, Rudy."

"It probably, Katie, has something to do with the case we're working on for Ajax," he said. "Those Wisemann drawings are worth quite a bit. Killing me would eliminate some of the competition."

"Where's your twerp partner?"

"Elsewhere."

Kate sighed again. "I can hold you on a whole shitpot of charges," she told him. "In fact, I may have to."

"If you let me slip away to New Paltz, *cara*, I promise I'll come back in a few days and explain all."

"Where the hell is New Paltz?"

"In New York State, on the banks of the majestic Hudson. A well-known college town."

"What's in New Paltz, besides a college?"

"Some answers, I think."

"I'll see what I can do."

Navarro grinned. "What time do you get off work?"

"What's this? An invitation?"

He shrugged. "I missed my movie, and I lost my yogurt. I have to have something to do in my room."

She laughed. "You know, if you weren't so charming, you'd... Okay, go on up. I'll be up to see you in an hour or so."

Rising, he bowed and took her hand. He touched his lips to her fingers. "*Buenas noches,* K.T."

"Same to you," she said. "And really, I am glad that son of a bitch didn't kill you."

20

THE NAKED DETECTIVE lit a cigarette.

Navarro, from his side of the bed, said, "I thought you quit."

Kate was sitting free of the blankets, with her knees drawn up. She seemed to be listening to the night rain hitting at the windows. "Actually I just, as it turns out, cut down from three packs a day to one," she said finally. "When I'm depressed it goes up to two."

"I used to have a similar problem with Mars Bars."

Exhaling, she said, "You're an evasive bastard."

Sitting up, and letting go of the sheet he'd been holding up close to his chin, Navarro said, "The problem is, *carita,* I always tell the absolute truth. Most people, however, can't handle the pure unadulterated truth, so they pretend I'm kidding."

"You sure as hell haven't told me the truth about your wife."

"I no longer have a wife."

"That's what I mean. You haven't explained what happened."

"Now I see why so many of the supermarket scandal sheets are published in these parts. Everybody hereabouts has an insatiable curiosity."

She took a long, slow draw on the cigarette. "Evasive again."

"Everything is temporary, Kate. Even marriage."

"Some of them last longer than others."

"True."

"You got hurt by all that, didn't you?"

"Very insightful, inspector. My wife walks out and you deduce it may've hurt me."

"Listen, when my husband left, I threw a party."

"How come I wasn't invited?"

"Wasn't that great a party, Navarro. Not worth coming all the way from LA for," she said. "Was she fooling around?"

"Yeah, with two sets of Siamese twins and a polka band. If you've ever come home and found your wife doing a brisk mazurka with two gents named Yin and Yang, then you know what real heartbreak can be."

"She did, didn't she?"

"I wish I had a Mars Bar right now," he said. "Or even that godawful yogurt I abandoned."

"If I were your wife, I wouldn't cheat on you."

"I'm touched."

"The hell with you, Navarro. It's impossible to be sympathetic and sisterly with you."

"I'm an only child. Plus which, I doubt I'd have had a sister who was long and blonde."

Kate reached in front of him, snuffing out the cigarette in the ashtray on the bedside table. "It's the same gun," she said."

"*Qué?*"

"The automatic Ernie Quesada was using — trying to use on you. Prelim tests indicate it's the same gun that was fired at you at the Duneen household. We dug some slugs out of the woodwork there, remember?"

"Same gun," he said thoughtfully. "How come you didn't tell me earlier?"

"I have priorities. Love first, then shop talk."

Navarro placed his palm on her smooth, warm back and traced small circular patterns. "Anything else?"

"Not so far."

"And you're still going to allow me to wing my way to New Paltz comes the dawn?"

"Yes, but you're going to have to come back, eventually."

"I shall," he promised. His hand slid down to her left buttock. "Do you think there was once a place called Old Paltz?"

"Yes, in Bavaria."

"Your wife didn't really sleep with somebody from a polka band, did she?"

"I'd have to check the list."

"Smartest thing for me to do," Kate said, "would be to give up cigarettes *and* you."

"We only see each other every couple of years. That's not an addiction or even much of a habit, K.T." He eased closer.

"And so we bid a fond farewell to picturesque Orlando," Navarro said. He had the aisle seat and was leaning so he could get a look out of the window on his right. "Our hearts a little heavier, our — "

"Why was your policewoman friend at the airport to see us off?" Briggs was in the middle seat. His fists were clenched. His eyes stared straight ahead, and he was striving to ignore the fact of the plane's climbing ever higher into the morning.

Jenny occupied the window seat. "She's obviously fond of him."

"She is that," admitted Navarro. "And she wants to make certain I come back soon."

"Yeah, she did seem anxious about that. She was alluding to something that happened last night. What was that about?"

Navarro turned away from the view of the retreating ground. "I didn't bother to phone you last night," he said. "But somebody tried to shoot me."

Briggs sat up. "Jesus, and you didn't even bother to phone me?"

"I'm filling you in now. By the time I got through with the various police procedures it was late."

"Okay, so do you know who it was that made the attempt?"

"A hefty gent in a ski mask."

Jennifer said, "Marzlov. I knew he'd try something."

"Nope, this was a lad named Ernie Quesada. He's apparently a freelance heavy."

"How'd you identify the guy?"

"They just took his wallet off his body."

"Body?" said Briggs. "You shot the guy?"

"Yeah, but I was only aiming to wound him. I was anxious... Well, I was mainly anxious not to go on to glory while strolling by the swimming pool at the Orlando Rococco Hotel, but after that I was anxious to talk to Quesada."

Briggs said, "That explains why the clerk was giving us the evil eye when we checked out."

"Hell, it's not as though I killed one of their paying guests," Navarro said. "Quesada came from elsewhere to do me in."

"Then it wasn't Marzlov at all," said Jennifer. "Not at the Duneen house, not at my motel."

"And not waiting for me beside the old swimming hole."

"Couldn't it be that there are two guys going around wearing ski masks?" asked Briggs.

"Ernie had the same gun as the fellow at the Duneen house."

"I was wrong, then," said Jennifer. "Yet I was almost certain."

Briggs said, "If this Quesada's the one, then we won't have to worry about being bothered by the guy in the ski mask anymore."

Navarro grinned. "Absolutely," he said. "Now we just have to worry about who hired him."

21

THE AFTERNOON WAS gray and muffled. The fog closed in thicker and thicker around them as they moved inland from the broad Hudson River. The trees rising up on each side of the roadway were blurred.

"We ought to be spotting the Hound of the Baskervilles any time now." Navarro was sitting alone in the back of their recently rented car with his feet up and a manila folder open on his lap.

Briggs was driving. "The heater doesn't work in this damn car."

"It has other advantages."

"To you, maybe. I was against renting a 1970 Monte Carlo."

"A classic car, and one you don't often encounter at your average car rental establishment."

"It's a charming automobile," said Jenny, who was in the passenger seat next to Briggs.

"Exactly." Navarro made a pencil notation on a sheet of yellow paper in his folder. "You want to make a right turn on the next side road."

"I know how to find New Paltz," Briggs assured him. "I once dated a girl who was attending the SUNY campus there."

"Mona Hergesheimer," said Navarro.

"Yeah, that's right. How'd you remember her?"

"A pretty name is like a melody, and tough to forget."

Jenny laughed. "You two make a great team."

"You should've seen us in our prime." Briggs guided the big car off the main highway.

Fog came swirling across the road, tangling around their Monte Carlo.

Navarro closed his folder and dropped it back in his attache case. He deposited his mechanical pencil in the breast pocket of his jacket, swung his feet to the floor and set the case beside him on the back seat.

Briggs asked, "By the way, Rudy, why did you have to stop at my place before we headed across the Hudson?"

"I wanted to retrieve my gun."

"Oh." Briggs tapped his fingers on the steering wheel. "Are you anticipating further violence?"

"It's always safer to anticipate it."

They were passing through a quiet suburban area. On their left sprawled the campus of the local State University of New York.

"Doesn't have the character of Cal," observed Briggs.

"Lacks sufficient ivy," said Navarro.

Jennifer looked back at him. "What did you major in at Berkeley?"

"Several things, depending on the semester."

"He was best at Political Science," said Briggs. "Not much good at Art."

"I did pretty good in Anthropology, too."

"You never studied Criminology?"

"Not until I got out into the real world."

She nodded at Briggs. "You were always interested in art?"

"Yep, from the start. Even in high school."

"Jack was a child prodigy," added Navarro.

"Well, you outgrow that eventually," said Briggs. "It gets harder to be one of those in your thirties."

"You forget I'm familiar with your work." She took his hand. "You're still damn good, Jack."

"At commercial art, maybe," Briggs said.

"You keep undervaluing yourself."

Navarro said, "We want to turn left up ahead."

They parked in a small lot next to a laundromat and started along the narrow, down-slanting street. The fog was thicker here in the heart of town, and the low buildings seemed to float in it.

126

There was a secondhand book store with windows pasted over in local ads and announcements, a small, skinny shop offering nothing but hanging plants and a natural foods restaurant named Eggplant.

"Your kind of place," remarked Briggs.

"Hum?"

"Restaurant we just passed. Had a sign in the window touting the Veggie Du Jour and another promising twenty-six flavors of yogurt within."

"I'll have to find out if they cater to LA." Navarro slowed, pointed. "Here's the Magic Flute."

"And not a flute in sight," noticed Jenny.

The window display consisted of a glittery drum set and several dangling electric guitars.

A small printed sign on the glass door said *Closed For Lunch*.

"Little late in the day for lunching." Navarro trotted on beyond the music shop, heading into an alley between the Magic Flute and a secondhand clothing store.

"Wait here," Briggs told Jenny and took off in his partner's wake.

"I'd rather tag along."

Navarro was at the back door of the shop. "Somebody's forced this lock fairly recently." He drew out his revolver.

Very slowly he turned the handle and started pulling the wooden door open.

Fog drifted in through the narrow opening.

Taking a deep breath, Navarro pulled the door wider. It made a keening, creaking noise. After shifting from one foot to the other a few times, he held his revolver straight out in front of him, then followed it into the shop. Just before he vanished from view he made a stay-put gesture at Briggs.

Briggs clocked a full minute on his wristwatch before moving to the open doorway.

"Careful," whispered Jenny.

A very fat cat, pale orange in color, dozed on the topmost step of a short flight of stairs leading up into the shadowy back room of the shop.

"Can't be too much wrong in there." Briggs went up the steps.

"Over here, *amigo*." Navarro was at the far side of the dimly lit room, kneeling beside two large cardboard cartons and a harp. "This must be Hal Lewis, Randy's friend and confidant."

"Dead?"

"He only sleeps."

On the floor next to the base of the gilded harp, gagged and trussed up with strands of green plastic clothesline, lay a fat young man in his middle twenties. His eyes were closed, and there was a large, brand new bump on his pale, wide forehead. His hair was close-cut and the same shade as the fat cat's fur.

"There's no sign of any trunk." Navarro put his gun away and took out his pocket knife. "It was probably sitting over there, where those music racks have toppled over."

"Marzlov got here first?"

"Somebody did."

"That's his trademark, the green rope."

"The .45 automatic was his trademark, too." He started cutting at the cords.

"Meaning what?"

"Meaning two can use the same M.O. as cheaply as one."

"How does that hook up with —"

"Jack? Are you all right in there?" called Jenny from the bottom of the stairs.

"Sure, you can come on up. Watch out for the cat."

"We're friends." She was carrying the cat, which purred a rattling, wheezing sound.

On the floor, the young man who was probably Hal Lewis, the consignee of the trunk full of Wisemann originals, groaned. His large head began to tick from side to side.

"Lewis?" Navarro undid the bandana gag.

"My own damn fault," the fat young man muttered, eyes still shut.

"What is?" Navarro folded the knife shut and dropped it in his pocket.

"My own damn fault. Who in the hell are you guys?" He'd

opened his eyes, which were bloodshot and a very pale blue.

"I'm Navarro, he's Briggs."

"That doesn't mean a whole hell of a lot to me."

"We know Randy Sunn."

"I know him, too. And I bet that's the reason I got bopped on the coco." With Navarro's help and considerable grunting, Lewis sat up. He was puffing. "They took that trunk. Full of dope, wasn't it?"

"Didn't you look inside?"

"Not me. That would've made me an accessory to whatever crime that idiot is involved in. Who'd you say you were?"

"I'm Navarro." He took out his wallet, flashed his credentials. "He's Briggs."

"I knew it. I'm in deep shit, right? Randy ships me that stupid trunk and — what's it loaded with? Drugs, I bet. Then a bunch of... Colombian dopesters, probably, a gang of Juan Valdezes, busts in here and conks me."

"Did you see who hit you?" asked Briggs.

"Not actually, no," admitted Lewis.

"You keep saying *they*."

"Just a guess. I came back from lunch and *bop!* — something hit me from out of the shadows. It's never very bright back here, and on a glum day like this it's even worse."

"Basically, then, you have no idea who assaulted you?" Navarro perched on a waist-high carton.

"Basically, no. Would you mind not sitting on that? There's a drum inside."

"Excuse it." Navarro dropped to the floor.

"It's easy to wreck drums by sitting on them. I've done it."

"When did you get back from lunch?" Navarro asked.

"Is Garfield safe and sound?"

"This Garfield?" asked Jenny, placing the purring cat on the plank floor near the fat young man's feet.

"Yes. I was afraid they'd maybe slaughtered him or something."

"He's named after a cat in a comic strip?" asked Briggs, frowning.

"My mother christened him Garfield. She's a fan of that insipid strip." With further assistance from Navarro he got all the way upright. "She's the one who overfeeds him, too. She overfeeds everybody."

"Back from lunch," reminded Navarro. "When did you come back?"

Lewis glanced at his plump left wrist. "At least they didn't swipe my watch," he said, chuckling ruefully. "It was just about three-thirty. Boy, I was out cold for almost an hour."

Briggs said, "Then he's long gone with the trunk."

"Is that what's in it? Drugs?"

"Nope," said Navarro.

"What then?"

"Art treasures," Briggs told him.

"Is that what Randy's smuggling now?"

"You and Randy close buddies?" Navarro asked.

"Not exactly. Not close enough so that I'm an accessory to anything."

"He's dead."

Lewis blinked and swallowed hard. "What?"

"Randy Sunn is dead."

The fat young man started to cry. "Jesus, I've known him ever since San Francisco. I even played at his club, during its brief life."

"The Blind Lemon," said Briggs.

"You've actually heard of it?"

"Only by reputation."

Sniffing, he tugged a wad of folded Kleenex out of his pants pocket and sneezed into it. "How'd he die?"

"He was murdered."

"Holy Christ." Lewis looked anxiously from side to side. "Could you please get me that chair over there? I really think I have to sit down."

Briggs fetched the chair. "Here you go."

"Thanks." The metal folding chair groaned and skittered as he sat on it. "Who murdered Randy?"

"We're not certain," said Navarro.

Jenny said, "But I thought it was that man Quesada who—"

"Nix," suggested Navarro.

Harris slumped in his chair. "Was it the same person who hit me?"

"That's a possibility," conceded Navarro.

"Could one of you please telephone my mother?" he asked them. "I'll give you the number. I think I better go home right now and lie down."

Navarro said, "Tell her to stop by a doctor first."

Reaching up, Lewis touched at the bump on his forehead. "A concussion, maybe?"

"Best to check."

He chuckled. "That's great. Wait'll Dr. Reisberson sees this lump. He thinks I'm a hypochondriac."

Briggs glanced at his partner. "Are we at a dead end?"

"Not exactly," Navarro answered.

22

"ALL OUT OF eggplant?" Navarro picked up the silkscreened Eggplant Restaurant menu again.

The thin, dark-haired waitress tugged at her silver loop earring. "That happens sometimes," she explained. "Ironic as it may sound." She watched him as he contemplated the other dinner entrees. "Are you from Los Angeles?"

He looked up and grinned. "I am, yes."

She smiled to herself. "I figured."

Briggs asked her, "How?"

"His accent," she answered.

"This is actually," said Navarro, who was sitting across the olive-green booth from his partner and Jenny, "a San Joaquin Valley accent."

"Close enough," the waitress said. "I'm majoring in Dramatics and Popular Culture at SUNY. So I pay attention to regional accents."

"When you get out to Hollywood, look me up."

"Broadway's more where I'd like to end up," she said. "And I know I'm skinny, but character actors — which is what I want to be — don't have to be zaftig."

"What's your name?" asked Navarro.

"Susan Miller."

"I'll watch for it in the Broadway theater pages."

"It'll be there."

Navarro said, "I'll have the mock meatloaf."

Her nose wrinkled. "You don't want that. Try the stuffed cabbage."

"That, I'll like?"

"More your style."

"I trust you completely. Bring on the stuffed cabbage." He snapped his menu shut and handed it to her.

Smiling at him, she headed off for the kitchen.

"See, it happens everywhere," said Briggs. "Women in all walks of life and in every clime are drawn to Rudy like a moth to —"

"Mothballs," said Navarro. "Now let us turn to business. It seems likely that whoever glommed the trunk is probably transporting it across state lines to Dr. Kathleen Starlin of Boston."

Briggs said, "We don't know that for sure."

"I still want to check her out first. If she doesn't have the loot, then we turn to —"

"Maybe I can help out," offered Jenny.

Navarro made a go-ahead gesture. "All contributions gratefully accepted."

"I don't think Kathleen is likely to be in Boston right now." Jenny ran her finger along the side of her water glass.

"Where, then?"

"She has a little summer house in a small Massachusetts town named Cosgrove," she answered. "It's in a woodsy area, and not many of her friends know about it. She likes to go there and write. I've only been there once, back when we were closer and I was helping her out on her Wisemann researches."

"Whereabouts is Cosgrove?" asked Briggs.

"About fifty miles this side of Boston."

Navarro inquired, "You figure Doc Starlin is more likely to be holed up there?"

"She wouldn't have the trunk brought to her Beacon Hill apartment in Boston," Jenny said. "She has to assume that you know about her by now. But, as far as she knows, you have no knowledge of her place in the woods."

"You do, though," said Briggs. "And she may know you're with us."

"It's much more likely Kathleen and Marzlov think I'm dead,

or at least incapacitated." She took a slow sip of her water. "That cottage would be a perfect place for them to rendezvous and store the trunk."

Navarro looked out into the foggy, twilit street, then up at the spinach-colored ceiling. "You can guide us to the place?"

"Sure, after I take a look at a road map."

"Then we'll embark as soon as possible."

"You're going to hate me." The thin waitress had returned.

"Never, not as long as there are stars in the heavens."

"I mean because I insisted on your having the stuffed cabbage," she explained. "Except we're out of that, too. Bruno, our chef, is back there eating the last one now."

"What hasn't Bruno gotten to yet?"

She looked sad. "We have plenty of mock meatloaf."

"I'll take it," Navarro said.

"This is my fault." Jenny was hunched in the passenger seat, again unfolding the road map they'd purchased several hours ago back in New Paltz.

"Keep in mind," reminded Navarro from the back seat, "that we're using a map we bought in a secondhand book shop. It could be outdated."

Their Monte Carlo had halted off a rural side road. Briggs was out in the rain, at the end of the headlight beams, examining some weatherbeaten road signs.

"Here's where we went wrong," said the young woman, narrowing her eyes to read the unfurled map in the faint light from the overhead lamp. "We should have taken the Phelps Road Bypass, not Old Phelps Road. I'm sorry. I really thought I knew this part of Massachusetts better."

"That's okay," said Navarro. "I enjoy sitting here listening to the sound of rain of the roof."

"Cosgrove's back ten miles the other way," announced Briggs as he climbed back behind the wheel.

"We want the Phelps Road Bypass," Jenny told him, folding up the map. "My memory's not as good as I thought."

Briggs wiped his wet hands on his handkerchief. "Up to that point you were a pretty good navigator."

He started the car, swung it back on the road and executed a bumpy U-turn. The windshield wipers made a clunking squeegee sound.

"Marie Vermillia," said Navarro.

"Yeah, I was just thinking of her, too."

Jenny said, "What am I missing?"

"We were recalling something that happened in our junior year," said Briggs. "Marie's father owned seventeen furniture stores in Northern California."

"Eighteen," corrected Navarro.

"You knew her better than I did. Eighteen. Anyway, she invited Navarro and me to join her and some of her elite sorority sisters for a few fun-filled days in Carmel. Her family had one of its many homes there. Rudy and I drove down from Berkeley in his ancient Ford. It was on a rainy night like this, and we got lost. We took about sixty miles to do the seventeen-mile drive, and I was getting out looking for road signs all through the night."

"We didn't arrive until dawn of the next day," added Navarro.

"When we eventually hit the Vermillia mansion, we learned that the young ladies had changed their minds and flown to Bermuda in one of Dad's private jets."

"That's sad," said Jenny. "You might be manager of eighteen furniture stores if you'd connected."

"There are forty-one stores today, but Rudy was the one she really liked."

The rain got heavier. Far off across the rolling hills lightning flashed and crackled. Thunder boomed, and a sharp wind came rushing across the road.

"*Caramba*," observed Navarro.

After a few moments, Jenny said, "We're coming to the spot where we went wrong before, Jack."

He slowed. "Oh, yeah, I see it. Phelps Road Bypass."

The road was narrow and rutted and partially flooded at several points. The Monte Carlo splashed its way along.

"The car's doing okay," said Briggs.

"Proving yet again that it was a wise choice."

After they'd driven another few miles, Jenny said, "Off on our right any time now is the road we need, Jack. It's called Greim's Lane."

"There it is." Briggs turned into the lane.

It was even narrower, a quirky road that climbed up through wooded hills.

"There 's a dead end about a quarter mile beyond Kathleen's cottage," said Jenny. "We can leave the car there and walk back on foot."

"Slosh back on foot," said Briggs.

As they drove by what might've been a farm house Jenny said, "The cottage is less than a mile ahead. Better kill the lights, so we can sneak by."

Briggs switched the headlights off.

A second later, lightning flashed, illuminating the pines and maples they were passing.

"There's her place, in that clearing," said Jenny, excited. "And the lights are on."

"If Kathleen Starlin and Marzlov are here," said Briggs, "then our trunk ought to be with them."

"I have a feeling that it is," said Jenny.

The road ended, and there was nothing but woodland ahead. Braking, Briggs turned off the engine.

Jenny said, "I know a way we can sneak up on the house. We can go into the woods back down the road a way and there's a path that'll take us to the rear of her place."

"*Muy bien*," said Navarro, backing out of the car and into the hard rain. "You lead the way, Jen."

Jenny came around to the back of the car. "I hope I can find that damn path. Especially at night."

Briggs joined them. "All set?"

"Jennifer's going to take the lead."

"Be patient with me," she said, smiling. "I was only out here once before in my life."

"Proceed." Navarro stood aside.

Jenny took three steps along the muddy road.

Then Navarro moved up behind her, yanked out his blackjack and hit her hard, at the base of her skull.

23

HER LEFT KNEE hit the road, then her right. She went limp and started to topple face forward toward the ground. Navarro lunged and caught her.

Briggs sucked in air and rain. "What the hell are you doing, you crazy son of a bitch?" He jumped for Navarro.

Navarro came up with the unconscious girl in his arms, keeping her between him and Briggs. "Quiet down."

"Quiet down? Jesus, you just killed Jenny." His right hand turned into a fist.

"She's only out cold. I know how to sap somebody."

"That's it. Fuck you. We're finished." He dropped his fist and reached out for Jenny. "Give her to me. I don't want you touching her."

"Will you quit hollering." Navarro pushed by him and carried her back to the car. "Otherwise, the ambush is likely to go off as planned."

Briggs didn't move. "What ambush?"

Raising one knee and balancing the woman's limp body, Navarro let go of her with one hand and pulled the back door of the Monte Carlo open. "The one she's been leading us into," he answered. He bent and eased her down onto the back seat.

The rain hit straight down on Briggs. "You're trying to tell me that Jenny is planning to kill us?"

Ducking half into the car, Navarro tugged his attache case out from under her body. "I've been doing some more checking," he said as he opened the case and took out some strands of green plastic clothesline. "I figured there'd be some use for these if I saved them."

"You and your fucking checking. What are you claiming now?"

"Jennifer Webb — if she's still alive — is a plump lady of forty-five. Her father went on to his reward three years ago last Thanksgiving." Navarro, working rapidly, tied up the girl's ankles and wrists. "I should've gone after all this information right off, but I guess when she admitted she wasn't a Connecticut schoolteacher — well, I let myself be conned. For a while."

"I don't believe any of this shit."

Navarro shut the door on the unconscious woman. "Even so, *amigo*. She's not Jennifer Webb, no more than she was Jenny Deacon."

"Who do you think she is?"

"Seems most likely she's Dr. Kathleen Starlin."

"Oh, c'mon, Rudy. That's fucking impossible. We know Dr. Starlin is a plump woman in her — "

"What's your source of that information?"

"Jenny told me."

"I talked to the dean of the Boston Graphics College. Kathleen Starlin is an attractive woman of thirty-one, with long, brunette hair."

"There you are then, that proves Jenny can't be Dr. Starlin. She's only in her late twenties and her hair is — "

"People can lie about their age, Jack, and they can dye their goddamn hair." He started away from the car and down the rainy road. "I'm guessing there's just one guy lying in wait for us at the cottage. I'm going to try to sneak up on him before he realizes she's botched this."

"But, listen, Rudy." Briggs started walking beside him. "If she really is Dr. Starlin, then why'd she tell us all about Dr. Starlin and what she was up to?"

"Think about it, and maybe it'll come to you." Navarro picked up his pace.

Briggs said, "Okay, I did tell her that we knew this Dr. Starlin was interested in the Wisemann originals."

"Yep, and to keep us from digging any further into Dr. Starlin's activities, Jenny told us all about her."

"But she didn't have to tell us about the Nazi loot. It had nothing to...shit." Briggs thrust his hands deep into his pants pockets. "She told us because it'd make us trust her and let her team up with us."

Nodding, Navarro left the road and moved in among the high, dark trees. "It's times like this that I wish I hadn't been drummed out of the Boy Scouts before I earned a single merit badge," he said. "I can see, *amigo*, why you've had an unbroken chain of failed marriages. You don't know the secret of successful bullshitting. Every good lie ought to have a foundation of truth. And, further, when you realize somebody is likely to come across the truth on their own, you rush in and give them your version first. That's all Jenny—a.k.a. Kathleen—has been doing."

Stumbling along just behind his partner, Briggs said, "When I mentioned the letter from her to Randy Sunn, she started giving me a story about that."

"Exactly."

"And she told us about the map because she wasn't sure how much we'd find out about that on our own," said Briggs. "This way, by pretending to be sharing information—shit—she knew I'd come and tell her whatever we might find out."

"Yep."

Briggs said, "Nobody tried to kill her at the motel either, huh?"

"Just a fine example of the new vaudeville, *amigo*. One more proof that we were all on the same side."

"Something else occurs to me," said Briggs. "They've already got the trunk, haven't they?"

"Sure, it really was at the Magic Flute. And her accomplice, who must've left Orlando last night, several hours ahead of us, collected it after conking Hal Lewis."

"Once Jenny knew they had it, she could've simply ditched us."

"Now you can see why I took the precaution of rendering her senseless."

"Wait now, Rudy. I don't think I can accept what you're leading up to."

"Okay, then I guess it isn't true."

"But, shit, the only reason to bring us here is so they can kill us."

"Bingo."

"It's very tough to believe she'd lead us into a trap, so she and her lover could slaughter us."

"It's like Little Red Riding Hood teaming up with the Big Bad Wolf."

"Okay, I guess I am reacting like a rube."

"To some extent, yes."

"You found out about her when?"

"Couple of days ago."

"That's why you were so jolly about her coming along with us."

"Safer to have at least one of our designated assassins where I could watch her."

"But I spent the night with her alone. Suppose she'd been planning to kill me at the motel?"

"They weren't going to kill us until they had the Wisemann trunk for certain."

"I tell you, Rudy, I thought by now I was too old to be disillusioned."

"You're never too old for that," said Navarro. "Now let's hush up. We're almost to the cottage."

24

NAVARRO, ALL BY himself, walked up to the cottage from the front and halted about fifteen feet from the red-painted front door. The cottage was surfaced with shingles of a dark stain. There were three cement steps leading up to the door, and white shutters framed the two windows. Light glowed behind the striped drapes.

"Ahoy, inside the house," called Navarro through cupped hands. "This is an emergency. We better talk."

There was no response, no hint of movement. The rain kept hitting at Navarro, and he hunched his shoulders.

"C'mon, your wife's been shot," he yelled. "She's going to die for sure unless we make a deal."

Another wet minute passed. Then the front door was yanked inward.

"Who the hell are you?"

"You know who I am. I'm Navarro. You're wasting time."

The man framed in the open doorway was tall and wide, about thirty-five. He wore black, and his head was shaved clean. In his right hand he held an automatic.

"What are you trying to say about Kathleen?"

"She's going to bleed to death unless you get moving." Navarro took two agitated steps closer to the house.

"What happened to her?" He kept the gun aimed at Navarro's chest.

"Look, Starlin, I didn't mean to shoot her at all," he explained, grimacing remorsefully. "But, shit, when we were coming here through the woods—well, she realized I was on to her and she tried to run." He gave a sad shrug. "I thought I could hit her in the leg, but instead she took the slug in her back. Jesus, there was a hell of a lot of bleeding. My partner's back there with her, and he knows a little first aid. But, man, she's got to get to a doctor quick."

"You crazy bastard! You shoot my wife and now you try to —"

"Easy, Starlin," advised Navarro, his eyes on the gun. "You shoot me now and Kathleen'll die for sure. If Briggs doesn't hear from me in five more minutes, he's going to take her away and dump her."

"He won't do that. He's hot for her."

"Not anymore. Once he found out she'd...Hey, we're straying from the point. What you do now, Starlin, is haul out the trunk. You give it to me, and we'll bring your wife here so you can get her to a medic. That's the deal."

"Or I just shoot you where you stand, asshole," said Kathleen's husband. "Then I go into the woods and kill your partner."

"Sure, if you can find him. And if your wife stays alive that long." Navarro gestured to his right. "It's a big forest, *amigo*, and it doesn't take very long to bleed to death."

"She better not...ooof!"

Briggs had come into the cottage the back way, approached the distracted Starlin quietly and hit him with Navarro's black-jack.

"Looks like I did it right, huh?"

Starlin slumped, stepped out onto the cement porch and started to pitch forward.

Navarro sprinted, jerked the gun from his slack fingers. He grabbed his sap from his partner and gave the collapsing man two more whaps on the skull to be on the safe side.

"Yeah, not bad." He hopped back as Starlin fell in the mud.

"You're a font of surprises, Rudy," said Briggs, leaning against the jamb.

Crouched, Navarro was frisking the unconscious man. "That I am."

"Why didn't you mention to me that this guy was Jenny...was Kathleen's husband?"

"Sometimes you can get an overdose of information," he said.

144

"Small doses are best in some cases. Grab his feet and we'll haul him inside and wrap him up."

Bending, Briggs asked, "There's no Marzlov?"

"He is, like the Easter Bunny, a mythical character. Kathleen made him up to divert us." Navarro got hold of Starlin's shoulders. "When I did my checking, I found out that Dr. Starlin had a hubby, and that he fit the description she'd given us of Marzlov."

"He was the original guy in the ski mask?" asked Briggs as they hefted Starlin into the cottage parlor.

"The one who tortured the Duneen girl and killed Randy Sunn," answered Navarro. "Dump him on the hook rug in front of the fireplace. He's probably got some green clothesline around the house we can use to hogtie him."

"The Quesada guy who tried to knock you off was —"

"A local Orlando goon hired by the Starlins for the occasion. He dressed in a similar outfit and was given one of Starlin's untraceable guns — another bit of diversion."

"So on top of everything else," said Briggs, letting go of his end of Starlin, "I've been committing adultery."

"I don't think they even rate that as a mortal sin these days," said Navarro.

"This is terrific." Grinning, Briggs crossed the bedroom to the open steamer trunk. "The Wisemann originals really exist."

Several dozen original drawings were scattered across the pale blue spread of the spoolbed, the rest were still resting inside the trunk. The lamp on the bedside table wasn't wearing its shade.

Briggs squatted next to the trunk. "What a great smell the past has."

"They're real?"

"No doubt."

Pushing some of the drawings aside, Navarro sat on the edge of the bed. "Pop Starlin's been in here hunting for the map," he said. "Pleasant way to pass the time until he had to get ready to kill us."

"I don't think he'd found it yet, since none of those drawings on the bed has been split into layers. He doesn't even have a razor blade around."

"So we have to double-check all these he's gone through and then do each and every one in the trunk."

"Hold off on that." Briggs's smile widened. "I've been thinking about this. It's possible Wisemann didn't have quite the sense of humor I've always thought he did." Very carefully, he began lifting bundles of originals from the trunk, which had been lined with a now-faded crimson Spanish shawl. "His being a Nazi really upsets me."

"You have to learn to separate the art from the artist," advised Navarro. "Same would apply to those who admire your paperback covers."

"The happy few." When Briggs had all the bundles of originals piled around him on the hardwood floor, he sat down crosslegged in their midst. "Loan me your penknife to cut the ribbons around the bundles."

Navarro obliged. "What is it you have in mind?"

"Aren't you the same Rudy Navarro who held back all sorts of vital information from me?" He cut away the faded red ribbon from a pile of about twenty drawings.

"That was merely to protect your tender heart."

Briggs was leafing through the drawings, most of which were about a foot square. "Boy, look at this one."

"Is it the map?"

"No, but look at these ballerinas dancing with this alligator. It's beautiful." He held the drawing toward his partner.

"We have several of the key members of the Starlin clan tied up at various choice locations," said Navarro. "We must, the law being what it is, report all this to the local cops before too long. After that we have to alert K.T. McBride in far-off Florida, our boss in LA and lord knows who else. We really don't have time to savor every damn squiggle."

Briggs was admiring the next Wisemann drawing in the stack. "Wood nymphs. Great stuff. God, what pen technique."

146

"I don't want to spoil this esthetic experience for you, Rollo. But we have to speed it up, so let's start candling these."

"Give me five or ten minutes," said Briggs. "If my hunch isn't right, then we can check each drawing against the lamp."

"Do I have to guess, or are you going to confide your hunch in me?"

"God, look at this one. It's an alternate version of the one of the elephant charging the beer wagon on a Munich street." He flipped through several more of the drawings. "Try to appreciate what I'm feeling, Rudy. It's as though you'd come across a whole warehouse full of albums by Herb Alpert and the Tijuana Brass. Think of how excited you'd be."

"*Andale,*" urged Navarro.

Briggs undid a second bundle and started looking through the drawings. "I still can't accept the fact Wisemann was a Hitler toady. It just — Ah!"

"What?" Navarro stood.

Briggs held up a drawing. It showed a group of monkeys and alligators, all dressed as pirates, in the act of burying a casket spilling over with gold doubloons. Getting to his feet, he held it close to the raw light bulb. "Yep, this it is. You can see the outlines of a map."

"Wisemann's little joke, huh?"

"He did quite a few of these pirate drawings. I thought maybe he'd hide the map between the plies of one of them."

"I knew I was right buying you at that slave auction. Congratulations."

"Now what do we do with this map?" He held the pen-and-ink drawing out to his partner.

"No use confusing the local law." After hesitating a few seconds, Navarro took the drawing. "I'll look after it." Rolling it up carefully, he slipped it away inside his shirt.

"And eventually?"

"Alas, we'll have to turn it over to somebody official who can see to it that all those hidden art treasures get returned to whoever really owns them."

Briggs nodded. "I figured you'd do that."

"I seem to be incapable of theft on such a grand scale," he said regretfully. "We better go through the rest of these drawings. In case there's another hidden map."

"I wanted to look through them anyway," said Briggs. "It'll be my only chance."

"Do that while I use the phone."

Briggs sat down on the floor and reached for another bundle of Wisemann originals.

25

IT WAS NAVARRO'S second morning back in Los Angeles. The day was already hot, and the morning Pacific had a dim, hazy look. A gang of seagulls loitered along the shore, perched on a long, surrealist twist of driftwood or dozed in the wet water's-edge sand. They seemed gloomy and low of spirits.

"Up and at 'em," urged Navarro as he came running by. "There's all kind of garbage out there waiting to be conquered."

The gulls ignored his advice.

Navarro continued on his way, his barefooted pace and breathing even and regular. When he reached his landmark — the airline hostess's redwood sundeck — he noted that she was not there. Instead, a sunbronzed and muscular young man was lifting dumbbells enthusiastically.

He scowled at Navarro. "What are you looking at, shorty?"

Smiling amiably, Navarro turned around and headed homeward. "If that lout is living with her, I'm going to need a new milepost."

On the run back to his beach house he was joined by a shaggy mutt who earned $100,000 a year doing dog food commercials and was being considered for an upcoming series on the Disney Channel. Navarro was the only one of his fellow beach residents the dog would have anything to do with.

Stopping in front of his house, Navarro said, "If you get a chance, Speedy, bite the muscleman who's shacking up with the redhead."

Nodding, the mutt went off to chase seagulls.

On the threshold of his large, low-key living room Navarro hesitated, sniffing the air.

Relaxing, he called out, "Emmy Lou?"

The tall blonde came in through another doorway. She was wearing sand-colored jeans and a candy-striped shirt. "I had to use the john."

"You drove all the way from Hollywood for that?"

"You always look very cute when you come back from jogging. Your hair gets curlier for one thing."

"Actually, Em, I tend to be cute day in and day out. Why did you bust in here?"

"Your door was open." She sat on his sofa, crossed her long legs and smiled at him. "You're back to your bad habit of not paying attention to phone calls. So I thought I'd drive out." She reached into her canvas shoulder bag. "I have something for you." She held out a letter-size envelope toward him. "Wexler said to make this check out to you. You can split with Briggs however you want."

"I thought you already sent him his ten thousand."

"We did. This is a bonus."

Navarro dropped into the black canvas chair opposite her. "From whom?"

"The Ajax Novelty Company. It's another ten thousand."

He scratched his head. "Wexler is giving me and Briggs another ten?"

Emmy Lou nodded. "While you were down in Florida straightening out that murder charge," she said, resting the envelope on her knee, "all sorts of things happened."

"I was never charged with murder or even manslaughter." He stood up. "When you defend yourself against an assassin's bullets, that's not considered a crime."

"I forgot, you have a girlfriend who's a cop back there. So she must've gotten you off with the minimum of fuss."

"Explain about the extra dough." He started for his kitchen, but stopped mid stride, went over, took the envelope off her knee and then went toward the kitchen.

"While you were in Florida," said the Ajax secretary, trailing

150

him, "the trunk of Wisemann drawings was turned over to the Coulthard family. Actually, to the widow of Randy Sunn, whose real name, if you're at all interested, was Randolph Malzberg."

"Not at all interested." Navarro filled his electric tea kettle and plugged it in. "I'm learning a lot from your lecture, but not about the damn bonus."

"Being around Briggs always makes you come back even nastier than usual." She rested her buttocks against the edge of his butcher block table. "The Coulthards agreed to sell our client, Kingsmark, one hundred of the Wisemann originals for an unspecified, but apparently large, sum. He's delighted, even though he didn't get them all, and he sent along a bonus to Ajax. Although it wasn't big enough to make your share ten thousand dollars."

Navarro dropped a peppermint teabag into a mug that had *Roy Rogers* written on its side. "Did I also win a Guggenheim whilst I was away?"

"Wexler turned over the copy of that treasure map. Wow, imagine that — Nazi treasure! Anyway, he turned over the copy of the map you gave him to a connection he has with the State Department."

"I kept a copy of that map. So if they're planning any tricky business — "

"No, no. It's already been passed on to Washington. Through proper channels, they'll get it to people in Europe. Wexler is anticipating that Ajax will eventually receive some sort of honorarium from someplace for helping all this art to be returned."

Navarro set the Ajax envelope on the table. "Wexler must be anticipating a rather large honorarium."

Emmy Lou asked him, "Did your plan work?"

"Which plan?"

"You were going to reform Briggs."

Navarro poured boiling water in the mug. "I'm not sure."

"Care to bet on it?"

"You're a very cynical woman, Em."

She didn't respond to that. "Were you going back to work?" she asked.

"No, I'm still on leave. I always try to take a few days off after an attempt on my life."

Nine days later in Manhattan, Briggs was returning from an early morning run up Lexington Avenue. A black postman in uniform shorts descended the steps of the apartment building.

"Would you be Jack Briggs?"

Looking up at him, Briggs swiftly reviewed the list of creditors he still hadn't paid off. There were only a few small ones left, none likely to spring for special delivery.

"Yes, I'm Jack Briggs," he admitted.

"Got an insured package for you." He produced a flat, brown-wrapped package from under his arm. "Sign this."

Briggs took the package up to his apartment. It was from Navarro and felt to weigh about a pound.

Briggs had cleaned and rearranged his living room. His magazines and newspapers were shoved back against the walls, and an easel near the windows held a nearly-finished painting of some old men on a shadowy Florida porch.

Skirting the painting, Briggs sat on his woebegone sofa and started opening the package, using his thumb as a knife. The process took nearly three minutes, and his thumb got cut once on a staple.

He slid out what was inside. "Jesus, that's great," he said aloud, laughing.

Navarro had sent him the Wisemann original that had contained the treasure map.

Still laughing, Briggs carried the discreetly framed drawing to the mantel and set it there, then stepped back to admire for a moment.

At the sofa once more he dug into the package and came out with a letter and a check for $5,000.

152

The letter, in Navarro's neat handwriting, said, "*Amigo*, we got a bonus from the client and here's your fifty percent. After having the map extracted and passing it on to the proper authorities, I figured the drawing was now in the public domain. You've always wanted one, so here it is. All in all, we didn't do badly on this case. And I have a feeling we'll do even better on our next job."

The hand holding the letter dropped to Briggs's side. "Our next job?"